RUNNING WITH JACK SCISSORS

DJ HELLMAN

STORYPOP PRESS

First edition

ISBN: 979-8-9999883-0-0

Published by Storypop Press

www.Storypop.Studio

My dad passed away in 2020, just as I was learning to write stories. This book wouldn't exist without his quiet but unwavering encouragement to "finish it."

So Dad, this one's for you.

*And for those who've stumbled, scraped, and still kept going...
it's for you too.*

ACKNOWLEDGMENTS

I want to send out a big thank you to all who helped make this book possible. To my mom and dad who always believed in me even when I gave them good cause not to. To Jerry Fushianes and Mary Lane-Peot whose enthusiasm for this story and helpful critiques helped polish it into what it has become. To the Boylan Sisters - Alexandra Boylan and Andrea Polnaszek - whose grace, generosity, and love for this story helped us to see what is possible.

And to the entire gang who showed up on a cold Saturday morning to shoot the proof-of-concept video when this was still a script in development - Tiffany Saggio, Wriley Hoffner, Marissa Joyce, Amy Radloff, Claudia Neve, Peter Malinger, and Bonnie Hilt. Your kindness and dedication will always be remembered. Thank you all!

DJ Hellman

CHAPTER ONE

Sitting alone on the infield grass, a wiry sixteen-year-old with red hair tied back in a ponytail kept to herself. Around her, the other track and field athletes milled about between heats. The sound of their chattering filled the air. The latest high school gossip always spread like a virus at a track meet. But Megan Zane appeared immune to the contagion as she stretched out oblivious to her surroundings.

BANG! The crack of the starting gun cut through the cold, crisp air on this late spring afternoon in Arcadia, Wisconsin. It jolted Megan out of her trance. She looked up from the infield of the high school track meet to see runners sprinting to the finish line of the 100-meter dash.

Megan pulled her knees up to her chest and watched as the other athletes walked past her. She noticed the crowd beyond them in the stands and along the chain-link fence that encircled the track. Throughout the crowd she could hear parents talking and cheering on their student athletes. Squinting as she looked over the crowd, she hoped she might catch a glimpse of someone there to cheer for her. She looked the crowd over once. Then a second time. No one.

As Megan continued to stretch, a shadow hovered over her

blocking the late-afternoon sun. She looked up to see her team-mate, Kristy McDermott, standing over her, fists on her hips and arms akimbo.

"Hey, Maggot! Don't blow this for us."

Megan furrowed her brow confused by the rude interruption. "What?"

"You know what." Kristy snapped back. "Make sure you get me the baton. We need a clean hand off."

"Whatever," Megan replied rolling her eyes and shaking her head as she went back to stretching.

"No. Not whatever," Kristy continued. "Last meet of the year. We would win for sure if Coach hadn't stuck us with you."

Kristy's words stung, but Megan couldn't let her know. She continued to stretch not saying a word. Kristy huffed, turned, and ran back towards their teammates, Jennifer and Gloria. They would be running the first two legs of the 4 x 200-meter relay. Megan would be the third leg and Kristy the fourth.

At their last track meet, Megan had dropped the baton on the handoff from Gloria. It had cost them the race as they finished far back in the pack. In fact, it had been an entire season of stumbles, missteps, and humiliations. Butterflies churned in Megan's stomach as the fear of another possible failure weighed heavily on her chest. She took a deep breath and closed her eyes for a moment hoping this last race might be different.

A voice echoed over the loudspeaker. "Next up, the girls four by two hundred relay. Runners please find your marks."

Coach Hendersen, a fit woman wearing sweatshirt and base-ball cap with a whistle around her neck walked over to where Megan was stretching. "Megan, you're up next. Let's go!"

She stood abruptly. "Yes, Coach!"

As Megan walked over to find her place on the track, Kristy ran past her, turned back, and yelled, "Run fast, Maggot!"

Megan scowled but said nothing. In the distance she could see Kristy's father, a man in his 40s with thinning hair wearing a dark suit. He shouted directions as if he were the head coach, "You've got this, Kristy! Remember your form! You've got this!"

Megan watched Kristy as she nodded to her father. She recalled the days of years past when they would warm up together before competitions — that was until Kristy's father started seeing Megan as a rival. It was difficult to fathom that only three years ago, they had been such good friends. But that was back in middle school and before Kristy's father realized that a track scholarship could get his daughter into a top college – maybe even Stanford. Nothing, not even friendship, could get in the way.

Megan found her mark and crouched low with her hands on her knees. As she stood there waiting for the gun to go off, she thought to herself, *Grab the baton*. She repeated those words over and over trying to lift the feeling of dread that consumed her.

Nervous anticipation began building in Megan's legs and stomach as the moment of silence lingered. Then *BANG!* The starter pistol fired. Runners of the first leg sprinted down the first straightaway.

Jennifer set a fast pace, and by the time she handed the baton off to Gloria, Megan's team - Arcadia High School - was in first place. Megan's chest tightened as she watched Gloria barreling towards her. *Grab the baton. Grab the baton.* She repeated those words over and over to herself.

In a few seconds Gloria was close. Megan began to slowly take off down the track, her hand reaching out behind her for the baton. Gloria reached forward as Megan felt the baton slam into her hand. She clung to it with a firm grip. Success! With that Megan was off.

Like a coiled spring being released, Megan bolted forward and was soon at top speed. She was halfway through her two hundred meters, cruising along and moving well. She could see Kristy ahead of her waiting for the handoff. Megan was about to let herself smile at the relief she felt in getting the baton when her right toe caught the track. She stumbled.

In an instant, memories of the past rushed in flooding her entire body. Images of herself on a walking trail next to a ledge flashed through Megan's mind. She could see herself stumbling and falling toward the ledge. In another instant, the memory was gone, but the feelings of panic and terror continued to course through her veins. Megan tried to regain her focus. But she could not stop hyperventilating. The harder she tried the more difficult it was to get her breathing under control.

Slowing down she struggled to regain her pace. The crowd's moans pierced her already scrambled mix of emotions. She tried to get her stride back, but her legs now felt like lead weights. Three of the other runners flew past her.

Megan struggled to regain her stride. Ahead of her she could see Kristy upset and screaming, "Come on!"

As Megan got close to Kristy, she could see her teammate's outstretched hand. Megan reached out to give the baton to Kristy. She missed. She tried again. Another miss. Finally, Kristy turned and grabbed the baton out of Megan's hand and was off.

Megan slowly came to a stop as she watched Kristy tear up the track. But no amount of speed could make up for Megan's stumble. Last place.

Megan stood there alone on the track staring down at her shoes. She tried in vain to shut out the low murmur from the crowd as her teammates' parents called out to console them.

"Nice job, Gloria!" shouted Gloria's mom.

Kristy's father chimed in, "Great run! Wasn't your fault!"

Megan finally looked up to see Kristy storming towards her.

"What the hell, Maggot!" she yelled. "Seriously! Last race of the year and you pull that?!"

Megan stood there frozen, taking her teammate's wrath. Coach Henderson came running over and got between the girls. "Okay! Okay! That's enough!"

"I don't know why she had to run with us!" Kristy wouldn't keep quiet.

Coach Henderson gave Kristy a stern look, "I said that's enough."

Megan stood there unable to say a word. Her entire body felt completely drained. Whatever energy she had left was used to fight the tears from coming. *Don't cry. Don't cry. Don't cry.* She thought to herself.

Coach Henderson hollered for the rest of the team to huddle up. As the other athletes gathered around, Megan could guess what her teammates were thinking. She felt trapped and alone in a sea of blame and resentment.

Coach Henderson talked to the girls huddled around. "I want to commend all of you for working hard this season. Through the ups and downs you never quit. So take pride in what you have achieved. For those of you going out for cross country in the fall, I strongly encourage you to train for the Labor Day 5k Race at the end of the summer. How you do in that race will tell me a lot about your commitment level for next year.... It has been a privilege to coach you all this season. And for you seniors, good luck to you. You will be missed. That is all. Enjoy your summer."

When the coach finished her speech, Megan slipped from the crowd as her teammates were greeted and congratulated by their parents. She knew there would be no one to greet and congratulate her. Of course, there was nothing worth congratulating.

Megan made her way across the field, grabbed her warm-up clothes and began to make her escape. As she skirted past the bleachers on her way to the parking lot, she heard a voice call out.

"Megan!... Megan!"

Megan looked up into the bleachers. She spied her friend and classmate, Riley - a sixteen-year-old wiry bundle of energy.

"You okay?" asked Riley.

Megan nodded quickly, "Yeah."

Another classmate and friend, Trevor, stood next to Riley and shouted, "It's just a silly race!"

Megan, her escape now clearly interrupted, let out an exasperated "I know."

Riley took her friend's cue and changed the subject. "You wanna go to the mini-putt with us on Sunday?"

"Maybe. Text me." Megan kept her answers short. She needed to get out of there.

"Sure thing," Riley answered.

With that, Megan waved to her friends and was off. She made a straight line for the parking lot where her little red Ford Fiesta was parked. She ran to the car, unlocked the door, and got inside. Alone in the silence, she watched as the other athletes and parents left the field together.

Among the crowd, Megan spied a little girl - a younger sibling of one of her teammates - skipping, jumping, and clicking her heels.

The image of the little girl took Megan back again. This time to when she herself was a little girl. She found herself back at the county fair holding a newly won goldfish in a clear plastic bag. She beamed with a smile as she looked at her dad and then jumped and clicked her heels. It had been a special father-daughter day out at the fair, and winning the goldfish was the crowning moment. She ran up to her dad and gave him a big hug.

"Love you, Dad," she whispered in his ear.

He whispered back, "Love you, Meggie."

As the memory lingered, Megan lost herself in a trance. Staring blankly out the window of her Fiesta she caught sight of Kristy and her father walking off the field staring right back at her. The contempt in their eyes jolted Megan back to reality. She quickly shifted the car into reverse, backed out, and sped out of the parking lot. The last track meet of the school year was finally over.

CHAPTER TWO

Megan drove through the town, glad to be rid of everything school-related. Not only had it been the last track meet of the year, it was also the last day of school. She had cleared out her locker earlier that day and said goodbye to a few classmates. Her overloaded backpack sat next to her on the front passenger seat as she headed for home.

A few minutes later, Megan pulled into the driveway of a nondescript beige ranch house that looked pretty much like every other ranch house on the block. She sat there for a moment dreading the thought of going in. Finally, she hit the button to open the garage door, stepped out of the car with her backpack, and headed up the driveway and into the garage.

She stopped at the door leading into the house and pressed the button to close the garage door. Taking a deep breath, she opened the door and stepped inside. The front living room was dimly lit. She called out, "Mom! I'm home!"

Megan could hear the television coming from the living room. She set her backpack on the kitchen counter next to an empty bottle of wine and a pizza box. Stepping into the living room, she found her mom watching a rerun of some sort of *Desperate Housewives* reality TV show.

"Mom?" Megan waited. Nothing. She spoke up a little louder, "Mom?"

Megan's mom, Amy Zane, looking disheveled and holding a glass of wine, kept her eyes fixated on the screen. She mumbled, "Hey. Pizza's on the counter."

Megan looked around at the mess that was the living room. Dirty dishes littered the end tables and an old sweatshirt was on the couch. She sighed and walked back towards the kitchen. "The track meet's over."

"Sorry I couldn't make it," Amy continued to mumble. "Work went long and I had a splitting headache."

"Yeah, well... it's over. You didn't miss much." Megan opened the pizza box and grabbed a slice. She took a bite.

Her mom finally turned away from the television and towards Megan. "I'm going to see Grandma tomorrow. She'd love to see you."

Megan tried to talk with her mouth still full of pizza, "Ugh. Could I have just one day to do nothing?"

"Alright," her mom answered. "I'll let Grandma know you're too busy to see her." She turned back to the television screen. "You still need to find a job for the summer."

Megan huffed as she grabbed her backpack and another piece of pizza. She stormed off to her room slamming the door behind her. Dropping the backpack on the floor, she sat back on her bed, took another bite of pizza, and set the rest on her nightstand.

As she slowly began to untie one of her running shoes, Megan's mind raced back to the moment she first put them on. It was at the shoe store with her dad. He stood there in anticipation as she laced them up. They smelled brand-new then.

"Well, Meggie? How do they feel?" he asked.

"Hold your horses," Megan replied with a smile. "Let me get them on."

She finished lacing them and stood up. She took a couple of steps as her dad stood there grinning. "Well?"

"They're perfect," she answered. "But are you sure? Look at the price!"

"Hey. Don't you worry about that."

Megan looked down at the shoes and then up at her dad. She ran to him and threw her arms around him, swallowed up in his embrace. "Thank you, Dad," she whispered. "Thank you."

As quickly as it came, the memory was gone. Megan continued to untie her running shoes. She slowly slipped them off and placed the shoes next to her closet. She went back to her bed and lay down, her eyes staring at the ceiling.

A tear slowly formed at the corner of her eye. It escaped, sliding down her temple and along her cheek. She closed her eyes tight determined not to let any more get away. But it was no use. The tears came.

Megan finally opened her eyes and whispered, "I miss you, Dad."

CHAPTER THREE

A loud knock at the door jolted Megan out of a deep sleep. She slowly raised her head and looked around the room. The sun was breaking through the window. Morning. She lay her head back down on her pillow. Her eyes fell shut still half asleep.

Another loud knock at the door and Megan lurched forward sitting straight up. Now she was awake. "Yeah?"

"Going to Grandma's," came her mom's muffled voice from the other side of the door. "Sure you don't want to come?"

"Can't I sleep in just one day?" groaned Megan as she pulled the hair out of her eyes.

The door creaked open and Amy peeked her head in the room. "Grandma would love to see you."

"Just one day. Please?"

"Okay. Fine," her mom answered, a certain irritation in her voice. "Stay home. But it's already nine o'clock. Don't stay in bed all day."

"I won't," answered Megan in the same irritated fashion.

Her mom lingered at the door, her hand resting on the doorframe. "You need to find a job, Megan," she said, her voice strained with a mix of concern and exasperation and the burden of unspoken anxieties.

Megan groaned, "I know," and rolled over in bed, wrapping the blankets tight around her and burying her head into her pillow.

She heard the door close. Her mom was gone. Megan lay there, a mounting frustration invading her rest as she realized there was no getting back to sleep.

She pulled the covers off and sat straight up again, her hair an even more tangled mess than it had been moments before. She headed to the bathroom to fix her wild mane. A ponytail would have to do for now.

Megan headed to the kitchen and poured herself a bowl of cereal. She poured the milk until it was empty. Opening the trash bin, she stuffed the empty milk carton down into the already overflowing garbage bin. It was garbage day tomorrow and it was her job to take the trash out. She could do it later. She had all day.

Plopping herself down on the sofa, she turned on the TV. Flipping through the channels between bites of cereal, nothing interested her. The first day of summer vacation and she was already bored. Thoughts of yesterday's failure at the track meet swirled in her head. As she flipped through the channels, she finally settled on the latest reality show.

She sighed. "Time to zone out." Anything that distracted her from her own thoughts was a welcome relief.

After spending the morning and early afternoon on the sofa, Megan was once again thoroughly bored. She got up and wandered into her bedroom. She looked around the room wondering what to do with the rest of her day.

She spied her running shoes by the closet. Another sigh. Over on her nightstand sat a picture of her and her dad at a middle school track meet from a few years past. She picked it up in her hands to take a closer look, remembering the moment.

That meet was something special. She had taken a hard fall when she tripped on the last hurdle in the 100-meter. Her leg was bleeding. The coach had examined the injury and bandaged it, telling Megan and her dad she was okay to run the 1600-meter if she wished to.

Megan remembered feeling uneasy as she held her leg - not sure if she should race. She looked to her dad. He looked at her with determination etched in his eyes. "Finish it." That's all he said. Megan took her dad's determination and ran the race of her life, beating the nearest competitor by three seconds. It had been the thrill of a lifetime and the highlight of her brief track career.

Megan continued looking at the picture of her and her dad smiling together and Megan wearing a medal around her neck. A picture of a world and a time that no longer existed. Just a memory in her head and heart. She wondered if that would someday fade away as well. Then there would be nothing left of her dad.

She sat for a moment, her feet dangling off the edge of the bed still holding the picture in her hands. She looked back at the shoes. "Might as well," she said to herself. Megan set the picture back on her dresser and grabbed the shoes.

A few minutes later she was dressed in her running gear and headed out the front door. Locking the door behind her, she got in her car and sped off. She drove to the outskirts of town where the fields and forests began. About a mile out of town, she turned onto an old country road and drove for a couple minutes before finally turning onto a gravel driveway. She pulled up to a trail and stopped the car.

The trail was a hard gravel trail. It had once been an old rail-road track, but that had been removed long ago when the trains stopped running. It was one of the lesser known walking trails in the area. Here she could be alone, by herself, the way she liked to run. No one to bother her.

After stretching for a few minutes, Megan looked both ways and began a slow jog down the trail. The air was refreshing as the sunlight bounced off the spring green leaves. The first week of June was always one of the prettiest times of the year in the rolling hills and farm fields of Western Wisconsin. But Megan hardly noticed, lost in her thoughts as she headed down the trail. Picking up speed, sweat began to bead on her forehead and run down her face.

The track meet from the day before continued to play over and over in her head. *Run faster Maggot!* Kristy's words haunted her. Megan picked up more speed. Maybe... just maybe she could outrun Kristy's words, the track meet, her mom... her life. If only she knew where to run to.

Megan continued on the trail deeper into the forest. The old trees threw shadows on the darkened path before her. She reached the farthest point she'd ever gone. She kept going. Her thoughts seemed to be a jumbled mix of hurt, sadness, anger, and confusion. There was too much to process and not enough trail to process it.

Kristy's voice boomed in her head. *What the hell, Maggot!* Megan tried to shake it off. She ran faster, the sweat soaking into her hair and shirt. With only the rustling leaves and her scattered thoughts to keep her company, Megan thought she was alone.

As she rounded a bend, the sound of approaching footsteps on the gravel trail caught her off guard. "Groovy runner on your left!" a voice called out cheerily, breaking the solitude of the forest.

The strange voice startled Megan out of her daydream. She flinched and turned to look at the runner who had come up behind her, seemingly out of nowhere. She stepped to the right to get out of the way. Her toe caught the gravel, and she stumbled forward sending her mind reeling back to a flash of a memory. It played like a silent, slow-motion film - her stumbling, falling over a ledge. A hand reaching out for her.

Panic jolted Megan's entire body like an electric shock. She caught herself and stopped abruptly trying to catch her breath. She sensed the other runner go past her and then stop. Hunched over, she tried to gasp for air as she began to hyperventilate.

Staring down at the ground she could see the shadow from the other runner standing over her. She heard the voice again, "Are you okay?"

Still struggling for air, Megan looked up to see a strange teenage boy about her age standing there, arms akimbo, looking down at her. He had blond curly hair and wore a red headband. A faded and worn green and yellow University of Oregon t-shirt covered his chest. On his feet were a pair of strangely-colored ragged sneakers. Long tube socks with red stripes went almost up to his knees. And to top off the ensemble, he wore yellow shorts that were way too short - at least shorter than any boy should be allowed to wear. It was a bizarre sight indeed. Megan nodded still trying to catch her breath.

"Are you sure you're okay?" the boy asked with genuine concern in his eyes. "You looked like you were somewhere far away."

Megan took a deep breath, trying to steady herself. "I... I guess I was... just lost in my thoughts," she admitted, surprised by her own honesty. "But, I'm fine. Thank you."

"Forgive me, but you don't look fine."

"No, really. I'm alright," she answered still catching her breath. "I just don't usually... see other runners out here... You startled me."

"Sorry. Didn't mean to scare you." He paused for a moment then put out his hand for a shake. "I'm Jack. Jack Scissors."

Megan hesitated, an eyebrow raised in skepticism. "Scissors?" she repeated, the name hanging oddly in the air. She studied him, trying to piece together what kind of person would carry such a peculiar name. Despite herself, she extended her hand, curiosity winning over caution.

"Yep. Just like it sounds."

"I'm Megan."

Jack beamed a big, toothy smile. "Well Megan, it's nice to meet you. Do you run here often?"

"Yes... well, no. Not lately... sometimes." Megan's brain was still processing the sight before her.

Jack continued on with a big grin. "Oh. Okay. Wanna run with me?"

Megan paused for a moment. "Ah, No. That's alright. Just running by myself."

"You sure?" he asked.

"I'm sure. Running alone helps me think. Clears my head."

"Well, alright then. Enjoy your run." Jack high stepped his knees as he backed away from Megan still facing her.

She continued to stare at the oddity before her, so out of place and time, so... different. He was about to turn down the trail when Megan called out to him, "Hey! Why are you dressed like that?" The words escaped before she could stop them. But she couldn't help herself.

Jack, unwavering, grinned back at her. "Prefontaine!" he exclaimed, as if that single word held a secret she was yet to uncover.

"Prefontaine?!" Megan looked thoroughly puzzled.

Jack called out again, "Steve Prefontaine! What? Never heard of him?"

"I... I've heard of him," she lied.

"Well good!" Jack smiled a geeky smile, waved, and turned to keep running. Megan found herself waving back at the bizarre figure. In another moment Jack was far down the trail.

Megan stood there alone bewildered by the boy. "Prefontaine?" she asked herself. She shook her head and started back in the direction of her car.

CHAPTER FOUR

The sun was setting by the time Megan got home. Her mom was not back yet from her grandma's. She had the house all to herself. Running to her bedroom, Megan pulled out her laptop and jumped on the bed. Lying on her stomach, she pecked away at the keyboard.

A search engine appeared, and she began to type the words "Steve Prefontaine" saying the name slowly as she typed it. Up popped a picture of Steve Prefontaine followed by numerous search results about the famous runner. Scanning the Wikipedia article, Megan discovered the numerous track and field records set by Prefontaine. She was quickly becoming impressed with this amazing runner whom she had never heard of.

Megan wondered why she had never heard of such a talented and good-looking, long-distance runner. She continued to scan the article. Then she gasped. She read the words aloud, slowly, "Died May 30th, 1975. He was just 24 years old." Megan frowned, saddened by the news. "Aw! That sucks... No wonder why I never heard of him."

She continued reading about how Prefontaine had died in a car wreck. Scrolling as she read, Megan came to a video titled "Prefontaine 1972 Olympics." She clicked on the video and watched, her eyes glued to the screen. It was the 1972 Olympic men's 5000-meter.

Fascinated by it all, she watched as Prefontaine got boxed in for the first half of the race but then broke out and took the lead. Other runners passed Prefontaine, only to have him come back and take the lead again. "Go, go, go!" Megan cheered as she found herself caught up in the moment. But her excitement was soon extinguished as the American runner faded in the last lap and just missed the bronze medal, finishing fourth.

"Aw, shoot! I guess he wasn't that good," she whispered.

Just then the front door slammed shut. Her mom was home.

"Megan, you here?!" Amy shouted.

Megan snapped the laptop shut, jumped up, and ran to the kitchen. "I'm here!" she exclaimed greeting her mom.

Amy was already at the fridge pouring herself a glass of wine. She pointed towards the counter. "There's some fried rice from the Chinese restaurant your grandma and I stopped at. Should still be warm."

"Okay. Thanks!" Megan grabbed a fork out of the drawer and started eating the fried rice out of the box. "How's Grandma?"

"She's doing well. She misses you... She was hoping to see you."

Megan rolled her eyes at the guilt trip. Amy set her glass down tipping it slightly and spilling some wine on the counter. "Dammit!" She grabbed a napkin and wiped up the mess. She opened the cupboard door to the garbage container to throw out the napkin. She looked down at the overflowing garbage container.

"Can you please take the garbage out like I told you to?!"

"What? When did you tell me?" Megan shrugged and held up her hands.

"I'm sure I told you this morning."

"I don't think you did."

"You never listen to what I say." Amy's temper was simmering.

"I'm just saying I don't think you said it," Megan insisted.

Amy slammed her hand on the counter. "It doesn't matter! You know tomorrow is garbage day and that it's your job to take it out! I shouldn't even have to say it!"

"Sheesh! Sorry. I was going to do it. I just didn't get to it yet."

"Well, just do it!"

Megan put down the fried rice. "I'm doing it. I'm doing it." She pulled the garbage bag out of the container.

"You don't listen to me... You never listen to me," Amy muttered.

"I just got back from running a little bit ago. I was going to do it." Megan tied the top of the bag and took it out to the garage. She threw it in the large plastic garbage bin and slammed the lid. She opened the garage door and wheeled the bin out to the street.

Megan marched back into the house and ran to her bedroom slamming the door behind her. She flung herself on her bed and started to cry. Through the tears she whispered, "Dad, I can't do this. I wish you were here. I'm sorry."

CHAPTER FIVE

The next morning Megan was once again awakened by a pounding on her bedroom door.

"I'm off to work!" her mom yelled through the closed door. "You need to find a job so start looking for one!"

Megan had barely opened her eyes before her mom was gone. But when she realized it was morning, she popped up out of bed with an unusual burst of enthusiasm. She was thinking about the strange boy she met on the trail.

Would he come back? she wondered. Only one way to find out. She had to go to the trail again. But he would most likely run at the same time each day. So she would have to bide her time and wait until the afternoon. So out to the living room Megan skipped, a lively spring in her step.

She again plopped herself down on the sofa and began surfing the channels. Nothing. She turned it off and pulled out her phone. She checked her text messages.

Her friend Riley was already up and texting - *What are you up to today?*

Megan's fingers answered a short reply - *Nothing right now. Supposed to be looking for a job.*

A few seconds passed. *Still on for mini-putt on Friday?* asked Riley.

Yep. 7:00? texted Megan in reply.

See you then. Text me if you get tired of looking for work.

Will do, she replied, setting down the phone. What to do until the afternoon. She went to the kitchen and opened the fridge staring blankly for a few seconds. The box of wine caught her attention. She lifted it up slightly. Nearly empty. Didn't her mom just buy that a couple of days ago? She frowned and shook her head as she let the refrigerator door close shut.

She went back to the sofa and picked up her phone. She typed in Prefontaine and started watching more videos of the famous track star. She quickly lost track of time, and soon it was mid-afternoon. Time to get her running gear on. This time Megan showered first. She knew this seemed silly as she would soon be sweating and in need of another shower. But she figured *Hey, a girl should look her best.*

A few minutes later Megan was out the door and headed to the trail. She parked in her usual spot, got out of the car, and walked onto the trail. She looked both ways while stretching. No one was there. Standing on her tiptoes, she craned her neck to look further down the trail. Still nothing.

After another minute of stretching, Megan shrugged her shoulders and headed off down the trail. A few minutes later she was far along, sweat running down her face. Today her feet felt light as a feather. Maybe the girl had some natural ability after all – no matter what Kristy and her other teammates said.

The leaves rustled softly overhead, and the scent of earth and pine filled the air, grounding her in the moment. Megan breathed in deeply catching her second wind. She was in the zone when she suddenly felt footsteps coming from behind her. A familiar voice called out "Groovy runner on your left!"

Megan stepped slightly to the right as Jack Scissors ran past her. Once again he was wearing the ragged sneakers, long striped tube socks, a T-shirt, red headband, and those short shorts.

Megan ran faster to catch up. *Dang! Jack can move!* She finally pulled up next to him and glanced over at the boy. Jack turned and glanced back at her. Megan quickly turned and looked back down the trail embarrassed as though she was caught spying. Jack smiled and turned back to the trail as both runners continued their brisk pace. Neither said a word.

Finally, Jack slowed down to a walk. Megan was relieved. She wasn't sure she could've kept that pace much longer. She put her hands on her hips as she looked up and down at Jack's clothes.

"So why the 1970's retro look?" she asked. "I mean, I know you said you like Prefontaine and all, but isn't that overdoing it just a bit?"

Jack stopped dead in his tracks. "How can you overdo Prefontaine? And any decade with Prefontaine has to be cool."

"If you say so," She muttered.

"Yes. Yes, I say so," replied Jack.

But Megan couldn't help noticing his shoes. She bent down and gave them a closer inspection. There were splotches of yellow, blue, and brown on white sneakers and a retro styled "78" drawn on the side. "What's up with the shoes?" she asked with a quizzical brow. "And why the number 78?"

"I designed these myself!" exclaimed Jack as he held up his foot for Megan to take a closer look. "I call them my 78s after my favorite year. Do you like them?"

"Actually..." Megan said, examining the shoe. "I love that retro look. Did you color them yourself?"

"Uh huh."

"But why is 1978 your favorite year? And do I even want to know?"

Jack was more than happy to volunteer an answer, "1978 may be the coolest year of the coolest decade. You had Fonzie, Evel Knievel, disco, the Bee Gees and *Saturday Night Fever*." He struck the classic disco pose with one hand pointing in the air.

"Okay, whatever," Megan answered as she wondered what the heck was a Fonzie. Better off not asking, she thought.

Megan continued walking and Jack followed. "I've never seen you here before. Are you new in town?" she asked.

"Here for the summer visiting my mom," Jack replied.

"Parents divorced?" Megan asked.

"No. Just separated. When I'm not here, I'm with my dad."

"Sorry. I shouldn't pry." Megan wondered what had gotten into her. She usually wasn't this nosy.

"No. That's alright." Jack responded. "I have hope they will get together again someday."

Jack smiled that big toothy grin. Megan could only respond with a perplexed look as she furrowed her eyebrows. "Don't you think that might be wishful thinking?"

"Naw. Always good to have hope. Hope keeps us going."

Megan was shocked by the sheer optimism of the boy - a quality she no longer possessed. She looked down at the ground her voice lower now. "Guess I wouldn't really know."

"So what's your story?" Jack asked brightly. "You from around here?"

Megan lifted her head at the cheerfulness of his voice. She answered, "Yep. Born and raised. I live with my mom here in town."

"Where's your dad?"

She shuddered at the question and stopped walking. She searched a moment for the words before answering. "He died... a little over a year ago."

Jack's face was one Megan had seen on so many folks at the funeral who had no idea what to say to her. She knew what was coming next.

"I'm so sorry," he said shaking his head. "I shouldn't have pried."

"No. It's okay. I was prying too." Megan looked down the trail from where they had come. She turned back to Jack. "Hey, I should head home."

"Do you have to go?" he pleaded.

"I really should." She began to walk back in the opposite direction.

"Will you be here tomorrow?"

"Maybe!" she shouted as she walked further down the trail.

"I'll take that!" he shouted back with a thumbs up.

Megan turned and continued walking back to her car. Then she turned back to Jack who was still standing where she left him. "Nice to meet you, Jack!"

"Nice to meet you too, Megan!"

Both of them turned and ran off in opposite directions. Megan smiled to herself, glad she had taken that shower.

CHAPTER SIX

The next day was much the same for Megan. She awoke once again to her mom pounding on the door. The morning was spent channel surfing and texting friends while waiting for the afternoon to come so she could go running.

Before she drove out to the running trail, she stopped off at a couple of local fast food restaurants to fill out job applications. She figured she better find something so her mom would leave her alone.

After submitting the applications, Megan headed for the trail. Again, she stretched and looked both ways down the trail to see if anyone was coming. Again, no one. She frowned, then started off down the trail - the same direction she had gone the last two days.

The sun filtered through the canopy, casting dappled patterns on the trail ahead. Megan felt a nervous excitement building in her as she wondered what this day might bring.

She was a few minutes into her run when she heard the familiar voice behind her.

"Groovy runner on your left!"

Megan turned to see Jack pull up alongside her.

"You're back!" Jack sounded excited to see her.

"I'm back," Megan answered trying her best to sound apathetic even though she was glad to see the strange fellow.

Megan looked down at Jack's clothes and rolled her eyes. The same outfit as the other days with the headband, long tube socks, and short shorts. The guy seriously needed someone to dress him – except for the shoes, which were actually cool. Thank goodness no one else was on the trail to see such a sight. Her classmates would have certainly gotten a good laugh out of the spectacle.

They ran together for a couple of minutes, neither saying a word. Finally, Jack broke the silence. "So why do you run?"

"I don't know. Just something to do." It was a lie. She knew why she ran – to escape. Escape her mom, school... memories. But she wasn't about to admit that to a boy she hardly knew.

"Do you run for competition? Track? Cross country?"

"I ran both track and cross country last year," Megan answered.

"Cool! How'd you do?"

Megan hesitated for a moment. "Well... I finished in the half that makes it possible for the others to finish in the top half."

"Gotcha," Jack answered. "What was your running strategy?"

"Running strategy?"

"Yeah. Were you starting off slow and then coming from behind? Or getting off to an early lead? What?"

Megan sighed, "I started slow and stayed slow."

"Oh." Jack paused for a moment taking in her answer. "Well, next season you should train like Prefontaine."

"Oh yeah? How's that?" she asked.

"Just go for the lead from the start and never give it up."

"Didn't work too well for Prefontaine though," Megan mused. She figured her answer might get a heated response. And she was right.

"What do you mean?" asked an exasperated Jack. "He was one of the greatest runners of his generation!"

"Didn't serve him well in the Olympics," she retorted. "He faded. Didn't even get a medal." Now she had Jack wound up.

"But no one under twenty-five had EVER won the five mile!" Jack was desperate to plead his idol's case. "And he almost pulled it off! He was running on pure guts!"

Megan gave Jack a slight grin. "Can't say that I know much about Prefontaine. I just Googled him and saw him lose in the Olympics."

Jack slowed down to a walk and Megan matched him. He had to slow down to make his argument.

"Oh my gosh!" he started arguing again. "He won six NCAA titles, and he set fifteen American records in every distance from two miles up to the 10K. He was one of the best of his time. And he was only twenty-four years old when he died. Like I said, no one under twenty-five had ever won the five-mile race. He was just twenty-one years old when he ran in the Olympics."

Megan nodded conceding the points he made. "Okay, I take back what I said," she offered. "Prefontaine was the greatest runner... never to win an Olympic medal."

"Pretty much sums it up. But it wasn't just his speed." The excitement in Jack's voice was building again. "It was his attitude and the way he ran. He ran for the lead from the beginning of every race. He was going to win because he had more guts than the other runners. He once said, 'Somebody may beat me, but they are going to have to bleed to do it.'"

"Is that how you run?" Megan asked.

"Yep. And it's how you should run."

"How I should run?" Megan didn't see anything about Prefontaine's style of running that could be applied to her athletic ability... or lack thereof.

"Yeah. That's how you should run." Jack was jacked up. "Don't let other runners pass you. Make them fight for it as long as you can."

"Well, with the way I run, I may last a full sixty seconds in the lead."

"It's a start." He paid no mind to her negativity. "Then your goal is to just keep increasing the time it takes for them to pass you until you get to the point where they can't."

Megan shook her head. "I just don't think I could ever be that good."

"You never know how good you can be until you just go for something all out. You just gotta believe it's possible and then start."

"Yeah, I suppose." Megan paused and looked up and down at Jack. "But the only thing I believe right now is that you need some different clothes."

Jack took a step back in mock surprise and hurt, his hand over his heart, "What?! Moi?!"

"Yes, you can't wear that," she half laughed at his response. "People are going to think you're weird."

"Well, maybe I am weird," he returned her laugh as he stuck out his chest in mock pride. "Or maybe I just have an appreciation for a great runner and a great decade that others just can't... appreciate."

"Well, you go on believing that," she answered. "Whatever works for ya."

"Okay, I will," Jack answered with his persistent upbeat attitude. He thought for a moment. "You know what I believe?"

Megan turned towards the lanky guy standing next to her. "What? What do you believe?"

Jack looked right at her with the most innocent, hopeful grin. "I believe you might want to give me a kiss someday."

That was the last thing Megan expected him to say. She burst out laughing. "Wow! That's bold!"

Jack raised an eyebrow. "Too soon?"

"Try way too soon. Like... 'see-you-next-century' too soon."

"Fair enough," he said, hands up in surrender. "Can't blame a guy for trying to cross something off his bucket list."

"Add 'not getting punched' to that list," Megan replied, grinning as she jogged ahead.

As Megan reached the head of the trail, she turned back to Jack. "Well, I really should be going."

Jack clasped his hands together begging, "Hope you're not mad at me for asking for a kiss."

"I'm not mad," Megan grinned. "You're just... odd, is all. But I really do have to go. My mom will be home soon and I need to get back."

"So you're not mad at me?" the optimism in his voice perking up again.

"I'm not mad."

"Will I see you tomorrow?"

"Maybe... If I can make it." Megan wasn't making any commitments.

"Alright." Jack answered. He paused then turned to her again. "So no kiss then?"

Megan laughed out loud as she turned away and waved her hand up in the air as a goodbye. "Like I said, maybe next century!"

As she walked away Jack shouted to her, "Will I see you tomorrow?"

Megan continued walking away. She shrugged her shoulders. "We'll see!"

CHAPTER SEVEN

Megan was awakened by the usual knock on her bedroom door. It slid open and her mom peeked her head inside. "I'm off to work," Amy said in a voice too upbeat for such an early hour. "Don't sleep all day."

Megan made no reply.

Amy closed the door and then quickly opened it again. "Oh! And I talked to Sam Mahato at the grocery store. He may have a job for you. So be sure to stop in there and fill out an application."

"Mmm Hmm." Megan groaned.

Amy took one more look at the motionless clump under the covers before closing the door and heading off for work.

As soon as the door shut, Megan threw off the covers and sat up straight. Her mind was still on yesterday's run with Jack. *A kiss?* she thought to herself. *What kind of weirdo asks for a kiss from someone they just met?* She shook her head and rubbed her eyes to get the sleep out.

Once up, she went through her usual routine of eating cereal while flipping through the channels on the TV. She continued to ponder her conversation with Jack. Should she even go back there to run with him again? He seemed harmless enough. And genuinely kind. But wow! What an odd kid! The boy was certainly a unique combination of annoying and amusing.

After texting Riley back and forth about getting together for mini-putt, Megan walked back into her room and stared at her shoes. "Well, Dad, what do you think?" She paused for a moment. "Oh, what the heck!"

Megan changed into her running clothes, slipped on her shoes, and laced them up good and tight. Soon she was out the door and driving off down the street.

She stopped in at Mahato's Grocery first. Her dad had known the owner, Sam Mahato. Megan had met him briefly at her dad's funeral. But that day had been such a blur that she didn't remember much about him.

She walked in and asked the front clerk for an application. She was quickly handed one and filled it out. A couple of minutes later she was back in her car headed for the trail... and that oddball with the odd name, Jack Scissors.

Megan took her time stretching, looking for Jack. He was nowhere to be seen. She finally headed off down the trail alone. It was a hot, sunny day and she had no problem working up a sweat. Fifteen minutes passed with no sign of the blond-haired boy. *Hmm, maybe he scared himself away with that stupid request for a kiss*, she thought to herself. *Oh well. Too bad.*

Then came the familiar steps behind her. She was just about to turn to look when she heard "Groovy runner on your left!"

Megan slid over on the trail to make room. Jack ran up next to her and began to keep pace. Megan looked over to see Jack dressed in his usual style... or lack thereof.

"Ah, yes," said Megan smiling with a tinge of amusement in her voice. "The socially awkward kid who asks inappropriate questions and doesn't know how to dress."

"One and the same," Jack replied with his usual upbeat optimism.

"Well, thank goodness there's only one."

"Enough about me." Jack quickly changed the subject. "Are you going out for cross country in the fall?"

"I don't know." Megan sounded unsure of herself. "There's this 5k race at the end of the summer. Our coach wants us to train for it and run in it if we are serious about cross country. But, I don't think I'm that serious about running."

"Why not?" asked Jack.

"I don't know," she answered slightly annoyed at the impertinence of the boy.

"Well, you like it enough to be out here with me."

"Jury's still out on whether I like being out here with you," she teased with a grin. "But, yeah. I like running. But some of my teammates can be real bi... I mean jerks. They can be real jerks. I can't stand them."

Jack nodded. "You'll find that there are a lot of what you politely call 'jerks' in this world," he countered. "But what are you going to do? Stop doing something you enjoy every time you run into a jerk?"

Megan sighed as she found herself slightly annoyed again. She didn't like having to explain herself, especially to someone she hardly knew. And, yet, that made it easier to reveal a bit of herself.

"I don't know," she muttered. "There's just this one girl who just..." Megan slowed to a walk and Jack followed suit. Megan began to spit out what she really thought, "Ughhh! I can't stand being around her! She's just mean.... And she thinks she's the greatest runner ever."

"Is she?" Jack's face was its usual portrait of curiosity.

"She's good." Megan admitted. "She's fast."

"Well, then. This is your chance to show her what's what. You could run with me. I could train you."

"What?" Megan stopped in her tracks upon hearing the offer.

Jack stopped as well as they turned to face each other. "Yeah! I'll train you." Jack's voice was as excited as it had ever been. "I'll train you to run like Prefontaine!"

"No," Megan shook her head. "No way."

"Yes! It will be perfect!" Now Jack was getting revved up. "You let me train you to run like Steve Prefontaine for the summer and when you jump way out in front, the mean girl... what's her name?"

"Kristy."

"Kristy! Kristy won't even know what hit her. I can see the panic in her eyes right now. I can see it." Jack was looking past Megan, his eyes wide open as though somewhere off in the distance he could see Megan beating her arch nemesis, Kristy.

Megan felt unnerved by his confidence. "How can you see it? I can't see it."

Jack paused for a moment and stared intently into Megan's eyes, "Some things have to be *believed* to be seen."

Megan turned away flustered by the earnestness she saw in Jack's eyes. "Then I guess I'm not seeing it," she mumbled.

"Not yet," answered Jack undeterred. "But give me a month of training you and you'll start to see it. And then you will start to believe it. And then... Well, look out Kristy!"

Megan turned back to face Jack. "You're serious."

"You bet I'm serious."

Megan began running slowly again pondering the offer. "I don't know. I'll have to think about it."

Jack continued running with her. In a few more yards they came to a fork in the trail. A sign at the side of the trail pointed to the right with the words "Rocky Climb" printed on it. They had run right past the sign on prior days.

This time Jack stopped. "Let's climb to the top of the ridge! That would make for a great first day of training."

Megan shook her head fiercely, "No, I'm going this way." She pointed to where the trail continued on flat to the left. She could feel the tension building in her stomach. It felt like a thousand butterflies trying to escape. She hoped Jack couldn't see the terror in her eyes.

"Aw, come on." Jack pleaded. "Nothing ventured, nothing gained. Let's go for it!"

"No!" Megan's voice rose almost shouting. "I'm not going that way! You can go yourself."

Jack stepped back and put his hands up at Megan's outburst. "Okay. Okay. It's alright," he said softly trying to calm Megan's anxiety. "We can go your way."

Megan's shoulders relaxed and she took a deep breath as the torment subsided. She sighed, "Thank you."

"No problem," answered Jack matter-of-factly. "I take it you have a fear of heights."

"You could say that."

"I get it," he continued. "We all have something that scares us."

"Yes, we do." Megan answered flatly lost in her thoughts.

"I know something that is a lot less scary than climbing up those rocks."

Megan turned to Jack with an inquisitive look. Where was he going with this? "Yeah, like what?"

"Like giving me a kiss." He beamed with a mischievous grin.

Megan laughed out loud at the incorrigible boy next to her. "You're terrible!" she said as she smiled and shook her head.

"What? I didn't *ask* for a kiss," he answered putting his hands up. "I just said it was less scary than climbing that rocky trail."

Megan paused and stared directly at Jack for a long moment. "I don't know," she said in mock concern.

Now Jack looked worried. "Don't know what?"

"Those lips of yours..."

"Yeah?" asked Jack.

"Yeah," answered Megan. "They look pretty scary."

"Oh come on! They're just lips. I don't have cooties."

"How old are you?" asked Megan.

"Seventeen."

"Then don't worry. You won't be seventeen forever. I'm sure some girl will eventually want to kiss those lips."

Jack turned away looking dejected, "I don't know. Sometimes it feels like I've been seventeen forever."

Megan laughed. "I know the feeling." She turned back towards her car. "Come on. I have to get back."

"I'm going to keep running for a while," he replied. "Will I see you tomorrow?"

"Can't," Megan answered as she started walking back to her car. "I've got plans with some friends. Maybe Monday."

"Okay. See you then?"

"Maybe!" Megan paused for a moment. "Will you act normal?"

Jack shrugged his shoulders, "What fun would that be?"

Megan shook her head and smiled as she began the long slow run back to her car. "Later, Jack!"

"Later, Megan!"

CHAPTER EIGHT

Megan spent most of her Friday trying not to think about Jack. But as she paced back and forth between the living room and bedroom, thoughts of the boy invaded her imagination. She channel surfed. She lay on her bed covering her face with her pillow trying to get him out of her head. But the more she tried not to think about him, the more her mind conjured up images for her to linger upon – the two of them running together, talking together... Jack asking for a kiss.

Who does that? Megan thought to herself. Certainly no boy she had ever met before. None of her friends ever had a strange boy ask them for a kiss out of the blue like that. In fact, she never heard of that happening to *any* girl she knew. There had to be something off about Jack.

Questions swirled in her mind. Should she continue to run with him? Should she train for the 5k? Would he ever stop asking for a kiss? Blech! Could she trust him? Might he be dangerous? Surely if he was he would have tried something by now. All she could figure was that he was just plain weird.

And yet she couldn't deny that she was a bit fond of the boy. There was a certain cuteness to him as well. Maybe it was his smile. Maybe that tousled blond hair tucked under that head-band. Or perhaps it was that he was... What was it exactly? He was just so... What's the word?... Genuine!

That was it! He had no mask. No fake persona. Nothing to protect himself from others and the harsh realities of the world. That was a rarity in high school. Heck it was even rare among adults. And whatever peculiarities Jack possessed, Megan had to admit to herself that he was not hard to look at. And he was kind of fun to be with.

She could feel herself letting down her guard with him, being real with him in ways she would not let herself be even with her closest friends. And then he had to ruin all of that by asking for a kiss. *Why couldn't I just meet a normal boy?* she thought to herself.

The thoughts running wild in Megan's head temporarily halted as a text from Riley appeared on her phone. She was to meet Riley and Trevor at the mini-putt in a short while. Megan texted Riley back, letting her know she would see them soon.

Megan quickly showered and got ready to go. As she was heading out of her bedroom, she caught a glimpse of her running shoes out of the corner of her eye. She stopped and stared for a long moment at the shoes. Megan didn't want to admit it, but there was more than a little bit of her that would have rather gone running. She did her best to toss that thought aside and headed to the mini-putt course to see her friends.

Riley and Trevor were waiting for her when she arrived.

"Well, there she is." Riley exclaimed as Megan got out of her car. "I was beginning to wonder if I had an imaginary friend."

"Nope. I'm real," replied Megan.

"Good. Had me worried there." Riley knew how to tease her friend.

Megan stood in front of her two longest and best friends. "Hey, Trevor. How's summer treating you?"

"Good. Good," he stammered, rubbing the back of his neck. "And, uh... you, Megan? How's your summer going?"

"Well..." she paused and thought for a moment. "Uneventful, as usual."

"Same here," he answered. "Just working most days at my dad's auto shop. Keeps me out of trouble."

"You two live truly boring lives," Riley interrupted. "Come on. Let's get our putters. You two are about to get your asses kicked."

"No girl's going to kick my ass," answered Trevor.

Megan laughed. "Well, then. It's game on."

Soon enough the three friends were putting golf balls around the mini-putt course laughing and joking with each other as they had done since grade school. Riley and Trevor kept trying to make impossible shots often getting penalty strokes for going off the course. Megan always played it safe keeping her ball on the greens and in bounds. But she could never judge distance.

Last hole it was all tied. Megan hit her usual safe but boring shot on the green but far from the hole. Trevor hit his ball hard. Too hard. It hit the board and went flying out of bounds.

Having seen the disastrous results of her friends, Riley lined up her shot and gave it a good whack! The ball was following the same path as Trevor's. But having taken a bit off her shot, Riley's ball bounced off the board making its way back to the hole until it dribbled in. A hole-in-one.

"Yes!" shouted Riley pumping her fist. "Who's the reigning champ of mini-putt?" She pointed to herself as she marched around in a circle.

"How am I going to live this down?" Trevor groaned in mock disappointment.

"Boo hoo, Trevor. You got beat by a girl." Megan came up and put her arm around him to console him. "But you'll be okay. I'm sure you'll somehow manage to pick yourself up and carry on."

Trevor tensed up a bit at the show of affection from his old friend and then tried to relax. He smiled, "Thanks, Megan. Your support means a lot on this dark day."

"Dark day?!" Riley retorted. "This is one of the greatest days in the history of my life. You two have been weighed and measured and found wanting."

Megan burst out laughing. "I had no idea we were in a medieval jousting match."

"Well, now you know," answered Riley. "Now let's go to Martin's Grill for a burger."

"I'm up for that," replied Megan falling in line.

The two girls began to walk off the course. Trevor held up for a moment. "Wish I could, but I have to get back to my dad's shop to clean up."

"Awe, come on," pleaded Riley. "Just one burger. It won't take too long."

"Sorry," he said. "I gotta go."

"Maybe next time." Megan replied.

"S-Sure. I-I'd love that." He smiled a quick smile at Megan and then went quickly to turn in his putter leaving the two girls standing there staring at him as he left.

"I'll call you!" hollered Riley. Trevor waved back and hurried off down the street.

The girls turned in their putters and started walking in the direction of Martin's to get a burger.

"He likes you," Riley stated flatly.

"What?" Megan asked pretending not to know what her friend meant.

"Trevor likes you. He told me."

"No way!" Megan's face was one of confusion. She blushed. This was something completely unexpected.

"What?" Riley asked incredulously. "Don't tell me you never noticed how he stutters and tenses up around you."

"I don't know. I just never figured that..."

Riley cut her off. "Yep. He likes you. And he's cute too."

Megan shook her head. "I just don't see him that way. We've known each other since third grade."

"Your loss then," answered Riley.

"Whatever." Megan felt exasperated. First Jack asking for a kiss. Now Trevor - her best friend since third grade - wanting to be more than friends. This was already quite the summer - and it was just the first week. "Let's just go eat."

CHAPTER NINE

As they sat in one of the booths at Martin's Grill, neither girl said much. Megan finished the last bite of her cheeseburger. "This might be the best burger place ever."

Riley answered, "Yeah, hard to beat a Martin's butter burger."

The two girls smiled at each other and then said in unison, "Mmmm. Butter!"

They giggled at themselves.

Riley slid out of the booth. "I gotta head over to the high school to pick up a book for a summer class. Why don't you come with me?"

"Summer class?" Megan asked, eyebrows raised.

Riley rolled her eyes. "Yeah, my mom's making me retake Geometry. She says I need all the help I can get to bring my grades up. She wants me to be able to get into Madison.

"Do you want to go to Madison?" asked Megan.

"I dunno." Riley shrugged her shoulders. "Come on. Let's go."

Megan slid out of the booth to join her friend. A few minutes later they were walking along the chain-link fence of the track behind the school. Some girls were on the track stretching and running. Megan looked closer. Her eyes widened, then she grimaced. It was Kristy, Gloria, and Jennifer - her teammates in the 4x200 relay.

Megan looked down hoping to avoid eye contact, but it was too late. Kristy came running over to them and grabbed on to the chain link fence dividing them.

"Hey Maggot! What are you and your loser friend doing here? Come to see what speed looks like?"

Megan kept walking. "We're just walking by. Never mind us."

Kristy followed them, her hands moving along the metal fence as she went. "Good. For a moment I thought you might be coming to train for the City 5k."

"Nope. Just walking by," Megan answered flatly.

"After you dropped the baton in our last 400-meter, it's nice to know you're finally quitting," jabbed Kristy.

Riley was quick to come to her friend's defense. "Shut up, Kristy!" she snapped.

"Stay out of this, Riley!" Kristy shot back as all the girls stopped walking. "I don't like teammates who make me and the rest of the team lose. Everyone else was like 'Be nice. Her dad died.'"

"Hey!" Riley shouted back.

Kristy was way over the line but wasn't about to stop. "But that was over a year ago. And you keep using it as an excuse to let the team down. Well, some of us *need* a scholarship. We don't have insurance money to pay for our college."

Riley moved in close to the fence just inches from Kristy. "You're lucky this fence is between us or I would -"

"Go ahead," Kristy interrupted. "But you know I'm right. I went easy on Maggot here for too long. Cost us the conference title." Kristy turned back to Megan. "So do us all a favor, Maggot, and quit. Don't do the 5k. You'd just be wasting yours and everyone else's time."

From the track Jennifer and Gloria were shouting for Kristy to return. "Come on! Let's go!" they shouted to her.

Kristy turned and began walking back to her teammates.

Riley shouted, "Hey Kristy!"

Kristy turned back, "What?"

"You're just like summer vacation!"

"Yeah?"

"Yeah! No class!"

Kristy's eyes narrowed in anger. She pointed at Riley, "Next time!" She turned and ran back to Gloria and Jennifer.

Megan stood there a long moment after Kristy ran back to her teammates. Her memory raced back to one afternoon in seventh grade, sitting on Kristy's bedroom floor surrounded by an assortment of lip gloss tubes, their latest friendship bracelets, some left-over beads, and an open shoebox with Kristy's latest running shoes.

"Dad says these new shoes will make me faster," said Kristy as she put on the shoes and laced them up. She stood up. "What do you think?"

"I think they'd go well with my khakis," replied Megan.

"Let's switch shoes," Kristy had said, slipping off her brand-new sneakers. "Yours must be faster the way you ran in our last meet. I'll trade for a week."

Megan had laughed. "You're crazy." She slipped off her shoes and handed them over.

"You're fast," Kristy had replied, lacing up Megan's shoes with a grin. "Fast girls wear cool shoes. But if you are going to be really cool you need one more thing." Kristy picked up her tube of cherry lip gloss and pulled off the cover. "Come here."

Megan had leaned forward and closed her eyes as Kristy applied the lip gloss to her lips. When she had finished, Megan tasted her lips, "Mmm, that's good. How do I look?"

"Cool," answered Kristy. "Now let's race!"

They'd raced around the block afterward, laughing all the way. Kristy's dad hadn't liked that. He told her to stop "goofing off."

But back then, Kristy had just laughed even more. Then Megan laughed. The laughter was contagious and soon both girls were rolling on the ground laughing in spite of Mr. McDermott's orders to the contrary.

But that version of Kristy was gone now - along with their friendship.

Megan tried to shake the memory loose as she turned to walk away. Her eyes welled up with tears.

Riley turned and put her arm around her downcast friend as they continued on. "Don't listen to any of that."

"Kind of hard not to," Megan answered wiping a tear from her cheek. "I hate Kristy. I can't believe we were ever friends."

"Well then, show her."

"What?"

"Run the 5k. Don't quit. Don't give her the satisfaction."

"I don't know. I just-"

"Just what?" asked Riley interrupting. She hesitated for a moment and then continued, "Look, I hate saying this, but Kristy isn't wrong about you since your dad died."

Megan took a step back, shocked at her friend's words.

Riley held up her hands. "I'm not saying you haven't got the right. I don't know how I would react if my dad died. I can't imagine. But I've felt like... like I'm losing you too. And I hate it. I don't want to lose my best friend."

Megan shook her head as she stared at the ground. She looked up at Riley and wiped another tear. "You're right. You can't imagine. I just can't... you just... you don't know everything."

Megan turned and walked quickly to the school with Riley trying to catch up.

———

That night Megan tossed and turned in her bed. Kristy's words played over and over in her head. Her anger grew into rage. She kicked her legs under the blankets in a fit of frustration. She hated Kristy. Hated her own life. And now even Riley was piling on.

But was Riley right? Should she run the 5k? It felt so pointless - hopeless to even try. It was easy for Riley to say 'go for it.' She didn't know. She didn't know how Megan's dad died. Not really. Megan had never told her the details of what happened. She couldn't tell anyone about that.

Tears streamed down her cheeks. She looked up at the ceiling and whispered, "Dad, please help me. I don't know what to do."

CHAPTER TEN

The next day Megan did her best to keep herself occupied waiting for her usual time to go running to find Jack. She flipped through channels, texted Riley, paced, and paced some more. It was no use.

She got into her running clothes, laced up her shoes, and was out the door. She was a good hour early. But she couldn't wait. She had to find Jack.

As Megan sped out of town, she could feel the anticipation building. She was nervous, scared, excited. Her stomach tied itself in knots. She took a deep breath and continued on.

Once at the trail, she got out and was about to start stretching when she was startled by the sight of Jack a little further down the trail also stretching. He was early too. Megan took a deep breath and walked towards the blond-haired boy.

Jack looked up from stretching, flashing his usual optimistic smile, "I guess I'm not the only one who showed up early."

Megan didn't mince words. She got right to the point, "If I let you train me for the 5k, what would it take to beat all the jerks?"

Jack stood up. "You mean Kristy."

"Especially Kristy." There was a new determination in Megan's voice, a steely resolve.

Jack put his hand to his chin thinking for a moment then put both hands on his hips. "Well, we will be doing sprints. And whenever we run, we will be going faster than you have run before for longer than you have run before. We need to get your heart and lung capacity built up to handle that. You will get one day off per week to rest your body. The other six days of the week you are mine."

Megan paused, thinking it through. "I have an interview tomorrow for a job at Mahato's Grocery. If I get the job, I'm not sure I would have time to train."

"When you're committed, you find the time." Jack wasn't accepting any excuses. "What hours would you be working?"

"I applied for the eight to four shift," replied Megan.

"Well, then. That's easy," answered Jack. "I'll see you here tomorrow after four... and every day after work."

Megan stood there silently. Her eyes narrowed as she stared intently at Jack. It was a lot of work. Could she really pull it off? She looked down at her shoes and then up to the sky. What would her dad tell her to do? Jack looked hesitantly up at the sky with her as if wondering what she saw.

Megan turned her gaze back to Jack with that newfound steely resolve, "Okay. Let's do it."

Jack let loose with a big smile, "Yes!"

"But no kisses!" Megan retorted holding out her arm, her hand wagging her index finger as though scolding a child.

"Aw," Jack responded in mock dejection. He then beamed a wide grin. "You may hate me some days. But you'll love the results. Let's go." And he took off running at a pace substantially faster than he and Megan had run on days prior.

Megan looked up to the sky again wondering what she had gotten herself into. Then she headed off to catch up to her new running coach.

CHAPTER ELEVEN

The next morning Megan awoke sore and tired. She was feeling the effects of the fast pace Jack set the day before. Doing her best to ignore the pain, she jumped out of bed, showered, dressed, and headed out the door.

A few minutes later she pulled into the parking lot of Mahato's Grocery Store. She walked through the sliding glass doors and approached the cashier. "Excuse me. Can you tell me where I can find Mr. Mahato?"

"Go through those doors," he said pointing to the back of the store. "Then to the left you will find his office."

Megan thanked him and walked to the back of the store. As she approached the swinging doors with an "employees only" sign on it, she noticed to her left an elderly woman struggling to reach a can of vegetables on a shelf.

Megan walked over to the elderly woman. "Here, let me help you with that." She reached up and grabbed the can of green beans and handed it to the woman.

"Thank you, dear," the woman answered. "You're very kind."

"No problem at all," replied Megan. "Have a wonderful day."

As Megan walked towards the swinging door, an older man in

his mid-60s wearing a Mahato's collared shirt and grocer apron followed her into the back room.

Megan turned to the left and eventually came to a small office with the door open. Inside was a small desk covered with a clutter of papers and invoices. On the wall hung a large calendar with various post-it notes attached to it. She peeked inside and then turned to see the man who had followed her.

"Can I help you?" asked the man.

Megan jumped back, startled. "Excuse me. Umm, yes. Mr. Mahato?"

"That's me."

"Umm, I'm Megan Turner. I think you spoke with my mom. I'm here for the interview."

Mr. Mahato looked down at his watch. "You are right on time. Come on in." Mr. Mahato gestured towards a chair in the office. Megan took a seat.

"It's nice to meet you, Megan. I've heard so much about you." Sam Mahato's voice was warm and inviting. "I know your mom, and I knew your dad." He paused for a moment. "You may not remember, but we met briefly at your father's funeral. Mark was a good man."

Megan squirmed in her chair. Hearing others talk about her dad always made her uncomfortable. "Um, thank you. And yes, I think I do remember meeting you."

Mr. Mahato quickly changed the subject. "So, are you able to show up on time?"

"Yep," Megan answered.

"And can you show up every day you are scheduled to work - assuming you are not sick?"

"Ah... yep."

"Any problems with stocking shelves?"

"Nope," she answered.

"Good. You're hired. Welcome aboard." And with that Sam Mahato stuck out his hand for a shake.

Megan stood up taking his hand looking somewhat bewildered. "So... that's it?"

"Yes, that's it," Sam answered. "You wouldn't believe how difficult it is to get people to show up on time and stock shelves." He paused for a moment and grabbed some paperwork from his desk. Turning back to Megan he asked, "So when can you start?"

"As soon as you need me to."

"I suppose tomorrow will be fine if that works for you."

"Works for me," answered an excited Megan. That was the easiest interview ever.

"If it wasn't asking too much, I'd ask you to start today. Had another employee not show up for his shift. I'm short-handed."

"I can start right now if you need me," offered Megan.

"Really?" he asked with a pleasant surprise on his face.

"Yes, really."

"You are too kind. That would be wonderful." He handed her the paperwork he held in his hand. "Here is all our paperwork for new employees. Fill that out while I find you a uniform shirt to wear. We'll have you stocking shelves in no time."

Megan sat back down, grabbed a pen from a mug of pens, and began filling out the forms. Sam went to find a uniform shirt for her to wear.

A few minutes later Sam was back holding a shirt in his hands. He traded the shirt for Megan's completed paperwork. He scanned it quickly. "Looks like everything is in order." He looked up at Megan and shook her hand again. "Welcome to the Mahato's Grocery team."

"Thank you!" answered an excited Megan. It had all been so much easier than she ever imagined.

"Oh! And I almost forgot," remarked Sam. "I have an app for you to download to your phone. It's my very own Mahato's Grocery app." He beamed with pride. "Anyway, you can use it to track hours, do inventory, and many other things on it."

"Okay. Cool."

"Yes, very cool indeed," Sam answered, delighted with his new hire. "You can go to the bathroom to change into your uniform and then meet me back here and I'll show you around."

Megan nodded and headed out of the office. Finally, she had a job. She was bubbling with excitement and relief. And maybe now her mom would finally stop nagging her.

CHAPTER TWELVE

Amy Zane sat on the sofa sipping a glass of wine and watching a rerun of Desperate Housewives. In an instant the front door burst open and Megan came running through the living room. Startled by the commotion, Amy sat up nearly spilling her wine.

She turned to see Megan rush to her bedroom slamming the door behind her. Amy set down the wine and walked over to the bedroom door. She could hear muffled shuffling and a drawer opening from within. She was just about to say something when the door flew open. Megan stopped with a jolt startling both herself and her mom.

"Sheesh!" exclaimed Amy. "You scared me half to death."

"Sorry," Megan apologized. "Just in a hurry."

"How did the interview go?"

"Good. Mr. Mahato put me right to work."

"Well, that's good." For once Megan's mom sounded pleased with something she said. "And where are you off to in such a rush?"

"Going running," replied Megan.

"Again?" asked Amy looking a bit annoyed.

Megan moved past her mom towards the front door. "Uh huh. Gotta train for the 5k."

Amy's face changed from annoyed to puzzled, "I thought you were giving that up."

"Nope. Change of plans."

"But what about supper?"

Megan opened the front door and turned back to her mom, "Save me some, and I'll eat when I get home."

Amy walked to the door as Megan made her way to the car. "Be careful."

Megan turned back. "I will," she answered and turned back to her car.

"And don't be gone too long!" shouted Amy.

"I won't!" she yelled back as she got in the car.

Amy slowly closed the door and walked back to the living room where her TV show and glass of wine were waiting. "She never listens to me," she mumbled to herself. She sat back down on the sofa and began sipping her wine.

———

A few minutes later Megan parked her car at the head of the trail. She jumped out to find Jack waiting for her. She noticed him holding something in his hands – a backpack.

"I'm here!" she said excitedly. "Came as fast as I could."

"Good," he answered with his usual cheerful grin. "Are we ready to begin?"

Megan returned the smile, "I'm ready. But, hey! I never got your phone number."

"No need. I don't have a phone."

Megan paused dumbfounded, "What?! How is that even possible?!"

Jack shrugged his shoulders, "My parents never got me one."

"But how do you talk to anyone?" she asked in disbelief.

"The way they talked to each other in the old days - face-to-face."

"But how am I supposed to contact you?"

"I'll meet you here every day when you are done with work," he answered. "And don't worry. My method of communication has worked for thousands of years."

"Okay," she said holding up her hands in mock surrender. "If you say so."

"Good. Now that we have that settled, here you go." Jack reached out and handed Megan the backpack. She grabbed hold of the backpack. As soon as Jack let go, the backpack, along with Megan's arm, dropped immediately to the ground.

Shocked by the extreme weight of the backpack, she asked, "What's in this thing?!"

"Rocks!" exclaimed Jack.

"Rocks?" asked a now thoroughly confused and somewhat worried Megan.

"Yes, rocks," repeated Jack beaming with pride. "Learn to run with these on your back and beating Kristy will be a breeze."

Megan stared blankly at the backpack. "You're serious," she said.

"Uh huh. Here let me help you." Jack grabbed the backpack and heaved it up onto Megan's back as he strapped it over her shoulders.

She slouched under the weight. "Really?" she asked hoping this might be a bad joke.

"Yes. Really," answered Jack in all seriousness.

Megan attempted to stand up straight, "I don't know if I can run like this."

Jack began to dig into the backpack, "Here, let me take a few out. This is your first time wearing it after all."

"You are too kind," she answered, her tone letting Jack know she didn't mean a word of what she said.

Jack ignored her as he continued to toss rocks out of the backpack. When he was finished he zipped it shut and asked, "Better?"

"A little," she muttered.

"All right then. Let's go!" Jack started off down the trail going slowly as he waited for Megan to catch up. With a certain reluctance, she began to pick up speed. With the heavy weight on her back she struggled to keep pace with her coach.... or torturer. She couldn't be sure which one Jack was.

Several minutes later the two runners were well down the trail. They turned around to head back. Jack was in the lead while Megan lagged behind drenched in sweat. Jack turned around to face her and began running backwards. "Come on! Keep up!" he yelled to her.

Megan struggled to reply through her heavy breathing, "I don't know... how much more of this... I can take."

Megan's legs felt like two oars rowing through wet cement. She didn't know if she could continue.

"We're almost done," Jack promised. "Run hard to the end."

Jack turned back around and took off in a sprint finishing where they first began. Lagging far behind came a ragged looking Megan, a sweat-soaked shirt clinging to her skin. As she reached the end of the trail, the worn out runner knelt down to the ground on one knee. She slowly untangled herself from the backpack and let it fall to the ground.

As Megan tried to catch her breath, Jack stood over her with his arms akimbo. "You need to get stronger," he said flatly.

Megan looked up at the figure standing over her trying to regain her senses, "What?"

"You heard me," he said, crossing his arms. "You need more strength. From now on you will be lifting weights three times a week."

"How am I supposed to do that?" Megan protested.

"Use the gym at the high school. You need to get stronger. And that means eating right and getting your sleep. No pizza. No fast food."

"But that's half of what my mom feeds me," answered Megan clearly not happy with her torturer... er... coach's latest order.

"Then you will have to make your own dinner," replied Jack clearly not sympathetic to any excuse Megan could muster. "You need protein, vegetables, and good carbs - rice, pasta, sweet potatoes. And before you get out here every day, eat a banana. It will give you a boost of energy."

"Not sure I can do all that," said Megan as she stared at the ground shaking her head.

"Trust me," Jack answered trying to reassure his student. "You can do it." Jack thought for a moment. "Here. Give me your shoe," he demanded.

"What?!" responded an incredulous Megan. "I'm not giving you my shoe."

Jack softened his voice, "Please. Trust me. Just give me your shoe."

Without taking her eye off of the boy, Megan slowly slipped off a sneaker and handed it over. Jack immediately pulled out three Sharpies of different colors out of his back pocket. He put his teeth around the cover of one of the markers and pulled it off. He turned it around to begin writing on her shoe.

Megan reached out and grabbed a hold of Jack's wrist. "Don't! My dad bought those for me!" Her eyes were wide with fear and anger.

Jack paused and didn't move. He spoke softly with tenderness in his voice "I know what these shoes mean to you. Your dad bought them for you. They are a sacred part of your past. I would never dishonor that. But these shoes are also about where you are going. And right now you need to be constantly reminded of not just your past but your future as well." He slowly removed her hand from his wrist. "Trust me."

Megan relented and stepped back sitting down on the ground. Jack went to one knee and then went to work on the shoe.

As Jack scribbled away on her shoe, Megan tilted her head as she wondered out loud, "So you don't carry a phone, but you have a bunch of Sharpies in your pocket. I don't get it."

Jack looked up for a moment, "What? A coach has to have

his Sharpies." And he went back to his artwork switching from one color of marker to the next.

Megan just shrugged as she waited for Jack to finish. Every moment felt like torture as she watched him deface her shoes with every mark of the Sharpie.

After several more scribbles, Jack finally completed his work. "There!" he said beaming with pride as he handed back the shoe.

Megan took the shoe as though it was made of glass. She turned it over slowly almost afraid to see what her new coach had done. But then she saw it. Along the side of the shoe Jack had drawn a fun and fanciful design. There were a couple of wildflowers, a fun smiley face, and words running along the bottom that read "Believe... and just start." Megan smiled at the drawing and words.

"So... you approve of my handiwork?" Jack asked.

"Yes, I like it. I like it very much." Megan answered as she stared at the shoe. "But why a wildflower? Why not a rose? I think if I was a flower, I would like to be a rose."

"Everybody wants to be a rose," Jack said in exasperation. "But the world would be a boring place if God made it all roses. God made some of us to be wildflowers. To show up in unexpected places. To surprise people."

"I don't think I'm one to surprise people," Megan retorted.

"And that's why I wrote those words. Believe and then just start. And when you do that, you'll surprise people. Cause you're a wildflower... just the way God made you."

Megan smiled at the thought as she put her shoe back on. She slowly stood up and brushed herself off.

Jack stood there smiling at his new student. "So, how do you feel?" he asked.

"Tired. I'm going home," Megan replied as she began walking back to her car.

"Too tired to give me a kiss?" asked Jack with a certain pep in his voice.

Megan turned back to see Jack with that big, geeky smile on

his face. She turned back towards her car shaking her head. "This is going to be a long summer."

Upon reaching her car, Megan turned back to see Jack right where she had left him. She called out to him with the little energy she had left, "You going to stay here?!"

"I'm not tired!" replied Jack shouting back to her. "Going to keep running for a bit!"

"Suit yourself! Have fun with your Sharpies! I'm going home!"

"See you tomorrow!" he answered and then turned and ran off.

Megan managed a tired, pathetic wave goodbye as she plopped herself down in the front seat of her car. Yep, this was going to be a really long summer... but maybe, just maybe, a fun one as well.

CHAPTER THIRTEEN

The incessant beeping of the alarm on Megan's phone finally forced her to move. She rolled over to her nightstand and turned off the infernal instrument. With every movement of her body, she ached and groaned. Struggling to sit up, she wiped the sleep from her eyes.

Megan made her way out of bed and stumbled to the doorway. She stopped as she spied her mom by the counter, still in her robe, cradling a mug of coffee. Her eyes were fixed on something in her hand—a picture frame.

Megan recognized that frame. It normally sat on a hutch in the corner. It held a picture of her mom and dad holding each other and smiling under a Fourth of July sky.

Megan looked on as her mom's thumb slowly traced the edge of the frame. A single tear rolled down her cheek before she could stop it.

Megan's hand slipped off the door frame making a slight noise that broke the silence.

Amy looked up and saw Megan staring at her. She quickly wiped her face and slid the photo into the drawer.

Megan walked into the kitchen pretending that she saw nothing.

"You're up early," said Amy, her voice strained but composed.

Megan nodded. "Yeah. Thought I'd go to the school gym to lift weights before work."

"The gym?"

"Uh huh. I need to lift weights to train for the 5k."

"What?" asked Amy suddenly perturbed. "I didn't think you were serious about cross country. Why the switch?"

"I don't know," answered Megan not wanting to give the real answer. "Does it matter? I just want to train for it. So I'm lifting weights."

"Well, I don't want you getting all big and muscular like those professional body builders," her mom retorted. "They almost don't look like women."

"Don't worry, Mom. That's not going to happen."

"Okay, whatever." Amy shook her head annoyed by this new revelation. "Don't listen to me. I'm just your mom. What do I know?"

The words stung, but Megan pretended not to hear them. She grabbed a banana and her backpack and headed for the door. "Gotta run." A moment later she was walking out the door.

Her mom set her coffee down and yelled, "Don't slam the -" The door slammed shut. Amy shook her head and lifted the cup up to her lips. She whispered to herself, "She never listens to me."

———

A short time later, Megan found herself at the school gym. That early, the place was empty. Just how she liked it. She had the entire room to herself. She preferred it that way as much of the equipment was all new to her.

She had been up the night before watching videos on the best weight routines for runners. She struggled as she got into the leg press machine. She had to drop the weight several notches before she could even budge it. She struggled to push with her legs. After a couple of repetitions, she had to lower the weight again and then performed a few more reps.

She started to sweat. "Jack better be right about this," she muttered.

After three sets she moved onto the next routine - hamstring curls. Again she struggled with the weight. And as this was all new to her, she had no muscle memory. Every rep was a struggle.

By the end of her workout she was exhausted and deflated. She was sweating more than she thought possible for lifting so little. The only good thing about her workout was that no one saw her. She showered and put on her work uniform and headed off for Mahato's.

Once at work, Megan was soon placing packaged meats in the open air coolers between the aisles of the frozen food section. She took a look at a steak and was taken aback by the price tag.

"Fourteen bucks?!" she said to herself. "Yeah, not happening." She put the steak back down and continued filling the cooler.

When she was done with the frozen meats, Megan's next task was filling the magazine rack near the front of the store. As she began sliding magazines into the rack, her eyes opened wide at the sight of Kristy walking into the store followed by Gloria and Jennifer.

Megan quickly ducked slightly behind the magazine rack while holding up a magazine to cover her face. As her eyes peered out over the magazine in her hands, she spied her nemesis perusing items on a shelf laughing with her entourage.

Megan became so engrossed with keeping Kristy in her sights that she completely forgot about displaying magazines in the rack.

"That's an interesting magazine display strategy," came a familiar voice from behind her.

Startled, Megan turned to see Sam Mahato standing there. "Oh! Mr. Mahato! I'm so sorry. I was just..." She paused unsure how to explain herself.

"Just what?" he asked sounding amused by the situation.

"Nothing. Sorry," Megan answered. She looked down at the magazines in the box on the floor. "I will get these done right away."

Sam looked up and saw Kristy and the other two girls still talking and laughing with each other. "I take it those are not friends of yours."

Megan looked up slowly at her boss. "No. Definitely not my friends."

"Well, no matter," he answered. "Hiding never makes a problem go away, okay?"

Megan nodded, "Okay."

"Okay then. Let's get back to work and never mind them." Sam walked away leaving Megan to finish with the magazines.

As she continued to put the magazines in the rack, Megan watched as Kristy, Gloria, and Jennifer walked out of the store. Maybe they didn't see her. Maybe she was safe.

She took a deep breath and let out a sigh of relief. She bent down to close up the remaining magazines left in the box to take them to the back of the store. She bent down to pick up the box. As she stood up straight, she looked out the large front window of the store to see Kristy standing there looking at her.

Kristy pointed at Megan and mouthed the words "I see you" and then walked away.

Megan's stomach dropped. How had she been seen? She gasped, turned, and fled to the safety of the back of the store. In a back corner behind several cases of canned goods, she leaned against the wall trying to settle her nerves. At least work would soon be over, and she would be training with Jack. It was the one place where the outside world wouldn't intrude.

CHAPTER FOURTEEN

After work Megan again made a mad dash for the trail. When she arrived, Jack was standing there again, waiting for her.

"Hey, you came back!" Jack exclaimed. He sounded surprised to see her.

"Yeah, I'm back," came the flat, monotone response.

"Wasn't sure you'd make it."

"Neither was I. I'm sore."

"Yeah," Jack responded nodding in agreement. "And that's why you need to eat right, get your protein, and get your sleep."

"It's fourteen dollars for a steak!" she protested. "I can't afford protein." She kicked the dirt with her shoe. "I could eat my shoelaces. Do they have protein?"

Jack smiled. "I don't think shoelaces are on the meal plan. Can't you ask your mom to buy that for you?" he asked. "I mean, she does feed you, right?"

Megan crossed her arms clearly not enjoying the conversation, "My mom isn't exactly thrilled that I'm training for the 5k."

Jack wrinkled his brow in disbelief. "Why not?" he asked.

"I don't know," Megan sighed looking up at the sky. She didn't want to discuss her mom. "Running was something I did with my dad. It was our thing." She paused for a moment looking down at the ground. After a long pause she finally looked up at Jack. "My mom and I haven't really talked much since he died."

"Oh, I didn't realize–"

Megan cut him off, "That's alright. It's complicated. Can we just run?"

Jack nodded, "You bet. Now let's make you fast." He proceeded to lift the backpack off the ground. The way he struggled to lift it told Megan that it was filled with rocks again.

Jack motioned for Megan to turn around. Megan complied but her downcast face revealed a certain reluctance. Jack spoke as he slid the backpack over Megan's shoulders. "Prefontaine said 'to give anything less than your best is to sacrifice the gift.'"

"I never said running is my gift," she answered.

"It's one of your gifts." He turned her around to face her and looked her in the eye. "Trust me. We just have to bring it out. And today you have one goal."

"What's that?"

He smiled his usual cheesy smile. "Keep up with me." With that Jack turned and went running down the trail at a fast clip.

"Wait up!" Megan yelled. She took off after him struggling under the weight of the rock-filled backpack.

Jack turned back to see how far behind Megan was. "Keep up!" he shouted.

Megan clenched her fists and stepped up her pace. Soon she was next to Jack matching him stride for stride. They continued at this brisk pace for another mile before turning around and heading back at the same pace.

The hot summer sun beat down on Megan as she labored to catch her breath. Her shirt was again drenched in sweat and sticking to her skin. Sweat ran down her forehead and into her eyes. The saltiness stung as she tried to wipe the sweat away so she could see.

While she labored for every step and breath, Jack looked like he was going for a stroll in the park. He looked over at the fading figure next to him and smiled. "Come on," he said encouraging Megan onward. "Let's finish strong."

He took off on a sprint leaving her in his dust. Jack stopped at the head of the trail as Megan again came lagging behind him completely exhausted.

"Annnd stop!" he yelled as she reached him.

Megan collapsed to her hands and knees trying to catch her breath. "I... don't know... if I can... do this."

"Sure you can," Jack responded in his most upbeat, positive voice. "That's another good day. Only 73 more to go."

Megan stood slowly, sweat marks streaking down her face. She took the backpack off her back and handed it to Jack. "Here... Take your rocks."

Megan stumbled back and took a few steps to the car leaving Jack to his bag of rocks.

As she continued to the car, she could hear Jack clear his throat.

"Soooo. No kiss then?" he asked.

Megan turned back to Jack exasperated and in disbelief. She looked down at herself. She pulled her shirt away from her skin and let it go as it clung to her again. "You have got to be kidding me. Look at me. I'm gross," she said, then pointed to Jack. "And look at you. You're not much better."

Jack shrugged his shoulders, "It's just part of running."

"Yeah, well, you promised no kisses. I'm going home." She turned back towards her car, took a few steps, then turned again to Jack. "You want a ride?"

"No. I'm going to run a bit further."

"Well, I'm done. I'm going home." She opened the door to her car.

"And that's when you will know you are ready!" he shouted.

"What's that?" Megan asked.

"When you can outrun me!" he answered. "That's when you know you are ready for the 5k!"

"Whatever. I'm going home." She got in her car and slammed the door.

"See you tomorrow!" he yelled.

Megan nodded, too tired for any more words. As she drove off she watched in her rearview mirror as the awkward kid in the red head band turned and ran down the trail.

CHAPTER FIFTEEN

The next morning the first rays of sun were beginning to peek over the horizon as Megan tied her running shoes. She grabbed her duffle and walked out to the kitchen. She left a note on the kitchen counter for her mom who was still asleep. Picking up her gear, she tiptoed to the front door quietly closing it behind her.

A few minutes later she pulled into the high school parking lot. Megan walked through the main hallway past the trophy case filled with plaques and trophies celebrating the school's champions from years past. She knew she would never do anything to be remembered in such a display.

She cut down a side hallway to the gym. As she got to the door she could hear someone already in the room working out. Megan slowly peeked her head in the door to see who was there.

In the middle of the gym she saw a girl on the leg press pushing hard and lifting a lot of weight - more than Megan could lift. As soon as the girl turned her head, Megan could see it was Kristy.

Megan gasped as she quickly ducked her head out of the doorway. She ran back down the corridor to the main hallway. She stopped at the trophy case and put her hand against the glass as she tried to catch her breath. What was she going to do? Jack ordered her to lift. But she just couldn't go in there with Kristy watching her. It would be too embarrassing. She certainly wasn't going to be lifting today.

She walked back to the car, unsure what to do. She ruled out going home. Her mom would be awake by now. After mulling it over for a few moments, Megan figured she might as well go to work a bit early.

Once at Mahato's Grocery, she clocked in and tried to do some stocking of inventory where she wouldn't be seen. But it only took a few minutes before her boss discovered her.

"Megan, what are you doing here so early?" asked Sam.

Megan flinched with surprise at the sound of his voice. "Mr. Mahato," she muttered. "I... I didn't see you there. I just got up early to go the gym, and..."

"Finished early?"

Megan hung her head eyes fixated on the floor. "I never started."

"Never started? Why not?"

Megan took a moment searching for the words not wanting to admit to her own cowardice. "Kristy... the girl you saw me hiding from the other day - she was there."

"Oh. I see," said Sam holding his hand to his chin. "So, what got you into lifting weights?"

"I'm going to run the Labor Day 5k," she admitted. "So I need to train for it."

"Is this Kristy running it as well?"

"Yeah. She's by far the fastest runner."

"So if you win, you will beat this Kristy." Sam pondered the thought.

"Yep," replied Megan.

"Well, I'm sure we can figure something out," said Sam, scratching his head as he thought it over. "But since you are here early, you can keep stocking the shelves."

"You bet!" said Megan, and she got back to work.

A couple of hours later, Megan was back in the frozen food section putting frozen chicken in the open air cooler. She was almost finished when Mr. Mahato walked over to her. He took the last wrapped chicken and placed it in the cooler.

He looked at Megan. "Follow me," he said.

Sam marched off to the back of the store with Megan close behind. He walked around the back side to where the pallets of extra food and beverages were stored. On each side of the pallets was metal racking for shelves and storing more pallets.

When Sam stopped, Megan looked at how he had configured the racking and pallets. There was now a metal bar placed across the racks. On each end of the bar hung a sack of potatoes.

Mr. Mahato turned and pointed proudly at his handy work. "Here you go!"

"What's this?" asked a puzzled Megan.

"This is your new workout room." Sam's face was beaming.

"Workout room?" Megan seemed more confused than ever.

"Yep!" he answered as he pointed to the bar. "This here's your squat bar." He got under the bar and placed the back of his neck under and against the metal bar. He grabbed the bar with both hands, and lifted the bar along with the bags of potatoes. He stepped away from the racking and proceeded to do three squats. He then stepped forward and set down the bar.

"See how easy that was? Now you try."

"Me?" asked Megan sheepishly.

"Yes, you. Go on."

Megan cautiously got under the bar. Placing the back of her neck against the bar, she lifted it along with the bags of potatoes. She stepped away from the racking and proceeded to squat down and stand back up. Once more and she set the bar back on the racking.

"Huh. It actually works," she said, a bit surprised.

"Of course it works," Sam was certainly proud of his invention. "And you can also work your calves by doing calf raises with a pallet." He proceeded to demonstrate by placing the ball of his right foot on the edge of a pallet while holding his left foot off the ground. He then did several calf raises while Megan looked on.

He then grabbed a bag of potatoes in each hand and did several calf raises on the other foot. "You can do them with more weight by holding these. Or you can do bicep curls as well." He stopped the calf raises and performed several alternating bicep curls with the bags of potatoes.

"Whatever you need for your workout room, I can rig it up here," he said. "So no more worrying about who's at the school gym, okay?"

Megan smiled, taken aback by her boss' generosity. "Okay... It's just that..."

"Just what?"

Megan continued, "It's just that... I'm supposed to be eating more protein to build muscle. But everything's so expensive. I just can't... afford it."

Mr. Mahato paused for a moment as he began thinking again. After a few seconds he looked at Megan excitedly. "Follow me!"

Again, Sam went marching off to another section at the back of the store with Megan following behind him. He came to a pallet with various food items on it. He picked up a can, looked at the date, and handed it to Megan.

"Here," he said. "It's a day past due. Still good to eat, but I can't sell it. So from now on you help yourself to anything on this pallet. And I'll be sure to have the meat department set aside anything for you as soon as it is one day past due for selling." He extended his hand to Megan. "Deal?"

Megan looked at the pallet of food and Mr. Mahato's hand bewildered by it all. She had never known someone to be so kind and generous to her. After a moment she extended her hand and the two of them shook on it.

"Deal!" said Megan unable to contain her smile. "Thank you, Mr. Mahato! Thank you!"

"My pleasure. We have to get you strong if you are going to beat that Kristy."

Megan smiled even bigger. "Yes sir!"

CHAPTER SIXTEEN

As Megan drove the short distance home from work, she was struck again by the kindness and generosity of Mr. Mahato. The year since her dad died had been one long stretch of gray. Mr. Mahato was an unexpected ray of sunshine in all that darkness.

Megan looked over at a bag of groceries in the seat next to her - a gift of out-of-date food from her boss. She thought about her upcoming run with Jack... and the rocks. Ugh! She wasn't looking forward to the rocks. But she found Jack's company amusing, even enjoyable. Perhaps another unexpected ray of sunshine. She hit the gas to get home.

Moments later Megan rushed through the front door past her mom sitting on the sofa with a glass of wine.

"Hey, Mom!" Megan exclaimed as she set the groceries on the kitchen counter.

"What's all that?" her mom asked slowly turning towards the kitchen.

Megan started putting the food away. "Just some old food that Mr. Mahato let me take home for training."

"For training?"

Megan continued putting the food in the cupboards and

refrigerator. "Yeah. It's the day old stuff he can't sell. I need protein if I am going to be lifting and training for the 5k."

Amy stood up and walked over to the kitchen island, glass of wine still in hand. "I'm not taking free handouts just so you can run a race."

Megan rolled her eyes at her mom's attempt to rain on her day. "It's not a handout! Mr. Mahato was going to throw it out anyway."

"So he's giving you rotten food to eat? Great. Just great."

Megan could feel her blood in her veins begin to boil. "Mom! It's a day old!" she said, holding out one of the cans of food. "It's fine to eat. He just can't sell it."

Megan darted out of the kitchen and into her bedroom slamming the door behind her. She quickly changed into her running clothes and shoes and put her hair in a ponytail.

A minute later she was back in the kitchen where her mom still stood, sipping her wine. Megan grabbed a banana, peeled it, and took a big bite. "Gotta go run," she said, her mouth half full of banana.

"I bought some pizza for you here." Amy pointed to a pizza box on the counter.

In her rush to put the food away and get out to the trail, Megan hadn't even noticed the pizza box. "That's all right," she said. "I'll eat the food from Mahato's when I get back."

"What?" her mom asked, a look of indignation on her face. "My food's not good enough now?"

Megan was already opening the front door on her way out of the house. "Mom, I'm in training. Be back soon." She slammed the door behind her leaving her mom standing there with her wine and the box of pizza.

Amy grabbed the pizza box, opened the garbage container, and shoved the pizza into the garbage. The garbage was overflowing and she had to press down hard on the pizza box to make it fit. She slammed the garbage door shut and took a big drink of her wine. She set it down and stared at the front door. That girl never listened to her.

CHAPTER SEVENTEEN

As she pulled up to the trail, Megan saw Jack standing there waiting for her with his big grin - and that backpack of rocks. She sighed. Lugging around a bag of rocks wasn't her definition of fun. But right now it was better than being at home.

"Come on! Let's go!" Jack yelled out to her.

"Yes, Sensei," Megan replied with mock enthusiasm.

"Sensei Jack Scissors," he mused aloud. "Hey, I like that."

Megan knew the drill. She turned her back towards him as he slipped the backpack over her shoulders. She adjusted it and turned back to her sensei. "Lead the way."

Jack turned and began running. Megan followed. After just a few minutes the sweat was running down Megan's face.

Jack chatted away as they ran. "Prefontaine always said the key to winning a race of endurance was being able to take more punishment than your opponents. That was his key to victory. And it will be yours."

Megan spoke as best she could between breaths. "So the more punishment I can take... the more punishment I can give my opponents."

"You got it."

"So when I endure punishment..." Megan replied. "...like this backpack... or you asking for a kiss... I'm getting stronger."

Jack furrowed his brow as he considered Megan's words. "Well, the backpack for sure.... Didn't realize you saw me asking for a kiss as punishment."

"Oh, yeah," she answered. "It's punishment. And as long as you can handle the rejection... I can handle the punishment."

Megan turned to Jack and smiled. She picked up the pace and got out in front of Jack, who had to work to catch up.

"That's it," Jack continued. "Use whatever motivates you, I guess."

"Oh. You asking me for a kiss definitely feels like a punishment. It's a good motivator." Megan ran faster getting another step in front of Jack as he trailed behind.

Jack paused before finally responding, "Maybe that's too much motivation."

After several more minutes, the fast pace was taking its toll on Sensei Jack's pupil. Megan's legs strained under the weight of the rocks. She was having difficulty catching her breath while keeping up the pace. She began to slow and falter. But the end was in sight.

"Come on!" Jack said trying to encourage her. "Just a bit more! Push yourself! Almost there!"

Megan tried with all her might to make her legs move faster - to push them like the pistons of an engine - up down, up down. Jack pulled out in front. Megan struggled to keep up. She couldn't breathe.

They finally reached the end of the trail and Megan fell to the ground out of breath. Jack stood over her, jogging in place, like he was ready to go another mile. "All done?" he asked.

Lying on her back, Megan looked up in disbelief. At that moment Jack's positive attitude and smile were the last thing she wanted to see. She labored to breathe as she struggled to get the desperately needed air that her lungs craved. After several more deep breaths she got up on her knees. She was completely spent.

"So..." Jack broke the silence. "How about a kiss?"

Megan was too tired to speak. She shook her head and laid back down on the ground her chest heaving with every breath.

"Let's call it a day," said Jack responding to Megan's silence. "That's enough punishment for one day – rocks and kiss requests."

Megan, eyes closed and lying on the ground, nodded in assent. It was all the response she could muster.

CHAPTER EIGHTEEN

The next morning Megan was up early and back at Mahato's for another work out. Same routine. Same sweat. Same aching legs.

She went through her leg workout. It was a struggle. Her muscles still hadn't caught on. And the contraptions set up by Mr. Mahato lacked many of the design features one would take for granted in an actual weight room. But it was still better than having to try to duck and dodge her way around Kristy at the school gym.

She worked up a good sweat performing squats as she added several cans of vegetables to the bags on each end of the metal bar. She strained on the last few reps as sweat beaded on her forehead.

When her workout was finished she used a shower that Mr. Mahato had available for employees. Then she was out on the floor stacking the shelves full of canned goods and produce.

At the end of the day she punched out, changed into her running clothes at work, ate a banana, and headed to the trail. Bringing her running gear to work saved her time. It also had the added advantage of avoiding her mom.

A few minutes later she parked her car at the trail where Jack was again waiting for her. But this time he had no backpack full of rocks. Finally, an easy training day.

"No rocks?" asked Megan.

"Not today," answered Jack. "Today we are doing drills."

"Drills? What new punishment have you devised?" Megan wondered if the rocks might be better. At least with the rocks she knew what she was in for.

"Prefontaine was famous for his 30-40 drills," said Jack.

"30-40 drills?"

"Yeah. He would run 200 yards in 30 seconds, and then run 200 yards in 40 seconds. He would run a full mile like that."

Megan stood there for a moment doing the math in her head. "Wait - 5280 feet divided by three is what?" She calculated more numbers in her head. "Two hundred yards in thirty seconds? That's less than a 4:30 mile pace.

Jack smiled. "Let's hope you're as good at running drills as you are at math."

"I can't run a four and a half minute mile," Megan protested.

"No," replied Jack as he held up a stopwatch. "But you can sprint. And that is what you will be running today."

"Damn."

Jack tilted his head. "Was that 'Gosh I love sprints! Thanks, Jack!'?"

"Something like that," answered Megan. "Just an abbreviated version."

"Good! Let's go!"

A few minutes later Jack stood on the side of the trail holding his stopwatch in hand. Far off in the distance stood Megan.

"Ready?" he shouted to her.

"Ready!" Megan shouted back.

"On your mark!... Get set!... Go!" Jack clicked the stopwatch and the seconds started ticking.

Megan sprinted hard towards Jack. Her arms pumped straight back and forth. She knew not to waste any motion. A few seconds later she ran past Jack as he pressed the stopwatch again.

"Way too slow!" He yelled as Megan came to a stop and turned around. "Let's go again!"

A couple of minutes later Megan was at her starting position again. Jack called out the starting sequence - ready, set, go - again as he pressed the stopwatch. Megan raced towards him. She ran past him in a blur as he looked down at the stopwatch.

"More speed! Faster!" Jack was all business.

Megan tried to catch her breath. Sprinting was not her strong suit. Her lungs gasped for air.

"Let's go again!" yelled her tormentor.

"I... I need.... I need a rest," Megan pleaded.

"That's not how these drills work," said Jack. "If you are going to run like Prefontaine, you gotta go all out on these drills. Again." He pointed to the starting line. "Let's go."

Megan slowly made her way over to the starting line. Again she ran fast and hard. But she was slowing down. Jack called for her to run again.

A half hour and eight sprints later, Megan was a mess of sweat with dust and dirt sticking to her legs, arms, and face.

"Okay. One more," said Jack. "One more all out and we'll call it a day."

"No more," pleaded Megan. "I can't."

Jack walked up to her and spoke slowly, softly, not much more than a whisper, "Yes, you can Megan. This sprint. This is where winners are made.... One more. You can do it."

Megan looked up at Jack. If she couldn't believe in herself, maybe she could borrow his belief. She trudged over to the starting line and got set once more.

And once more Jack yelled "Go!" and Megan was off. She ran as hard and fast as she could. But her energy was gone. She could barely breathe, but she kept on running all the way through until she passed Jack and his stopwatch.

Megan went to the ground on her hands and knees as she

heaved and fought to get oxygen into her lungs. Jack looked down at her.

"Slow, but good effort," he said. "So, how about a—"

Megan doubled over and began to vomit.

Jack took one look and turned pale. "Okay, wow. Definitely not the vibe I was going for."

Megan managed a thumbs-up from the grass.

"Tell you what," Jack said. "Rain check on the kiss."

Megan could only shake her head as she continued vomiting. Jack turned away too grossed out to watch.

CHAPTER NINETEEN

The next several days were a blur of the usual routine. Early each morning Megan was up before her mom and out the door. Three days of the week she was lifting weights using the odd contraptions Mr. Mahato had set up for her. Other employees watched in amusement and some even joined in to spot for her.

Mondays and Fridays were upper body and back days – push-ups, pull-ups, and curls. She struggled at first to do a single pull-up. She had to stand on a chair just to do them. Push-ups weren't much better. She started on her knees and strained with all her might just to do five.

Wednesdays were leg days - squats, thigh extensions, hamstring curls, calf raises. Various bags with canned food in them were easily adjusted by removing or adding more cans. Megan struggled lifting with her legs as well. But this came easier than upper body as her legs already had some strength from all the running she was doing. Tuesdays and Thursdays were days for stretching and light calisthenics to let her body rest.

After each morning workout, she showered and completed her usual work shift. Her typical work routine consisted of stocking shelves, filling the magazine racks, cleaning the back room, and every now and then doing her best to hide if Kristy walked in the store.

At the end of each workday Megan ate her banana at work or home before heading off for another session of torture and punishment with Jack. She usually left for the trail straight from work. And on those days where she had to go home first, Megan was sure to avoid any lengthy conversation with her mom.

The conversations Megan did have with her mom were usually limited to reminders to take out the garbage and not slam the door on her way out. And when her mom had a glass of wine in her hand - which was most days - Megan tried extra hard to avoid any conversation all together. But if the garbage was full, there was no getting away from a blow up between her and her mom. Such was her home life.

When Megan got to the trail at the end of each work day, Jack was always there waiting for her - usually with a backpack full of rocks in hand. And whether rain or shine, the two would run together as Jack talked incessantly about Steve Prefontaine. And each day brought a new way for Jack to ask for a kiss and a new way for Megan to reject him.

After another lung-destroying run, Megan pulled the backpack of rocks off her back as she went to her knees gasping for air. With the backpack of rocks in front of her, Jack didn't realize the danger he was in when he asked for another kiss.

As soon as she heard the dreaded question, Megan reached into the backpack. "Oh, you want a kiss?"

She hurled the first rock. "Here—"

Then another. "Is—"

And then a final missile. "Your KISS!"

Jack ducked and dodged, the last one catching him on the shoulder. "Ow! Abuse!"

"Emotional resilience training," Megan said, dusting off her hands. "You're welcome."

"Hey!" cried Jack. "That hurt."

"Good!" There was no mercy in Megan's voice. Perhaps this

would put an end to Jack's endless requests for a kiss. But that was not likely to be the case.

On another day, a steady downpour drenched the ground. Megan thought for sure Jack would cancel the run. But since he didn't have a phone there was no way to call. So out she drove to the trail. And sure enough, there was Jack standing in the pouring rain holding the backpack.

So off they ran in the rain, the mud, and the muck. Jack still pushed a fast pace with Megan struggling to keep up as usual. While some puddles could be jumped, many were unavoidable. Both runners were splashed with mud and water as their shoes hit the puddles.

They laughed as they looked at the mess each of them had become. At one point far down the trail, Megan attempted to avoid a puddle. As she bounded over it, her foot caught the grass on the edge of the trail. She slipped, lost her footing, and went tumbling down in the mud.

"Are you okay?" asked Jack clearly concerned.

"I'm fine," answered Megan. Only her pride, and maybe her dignity, were bruised. She began to lift herself up. Looking up, she saw Jack's outstretched hand.

"Give me your hand," he said gently.

She reached out and placed her hand in his. In all their days together, this was the first time he had touched her, other than strapping on that dreaded backpack. She felt his strength as he lifted her up and she got to her feet.

"Here, Meggie. I've got you."

"What did you call me?" asked Megan taken aback.

"Meggie," replied Jack.

"That's what my dad used to call me."

For a long moment the two stood face-to-face with Jack still holding Megan's hand. Neither let go.

Finally, Megan said a quick "Thank you" and took her hand out of Jack's.

"Come on," he said. "We have a long way back. Let's pick up

the pace."

They ran hard back to the head of the trail. The rain continued pouring down. But Megan felt lighter and running was easier as she thought about the feeling of Jack taking her by the hand. His touch was both gentle and strong... and somehow reassuring. She wasn't expecting that. It surprised her.

Jack increased his speed and Megan matched him. The last hundred yards the two runners sprinted together. Reaching the end, Megan walked slowly in a circle trying to catch her breath. When she turned to look at Jack, there he was pointing at his lips with a questioning face hoping for a kiss.

"Seriously?!" asked Megan, half frustrated, half amused. "Look at me." She looked down at herself. "And look at you. We are both a mess."

"I don't know," he said while smiling at Megan. "Just seems like it would be romantic to kiss someone in the pouring rain."

Megan looked up and shook her head. "Ugh! You can be so infuriating sometimes!"

Jack shrugged his shoulders. "You don't get what you want in life if you don't ask."

"Whatever," she answered. "I'm going home. Let me guess - you don't need a ride."

"Nope. I'll see you tomorrow."

She walked slowly to her car and waved, "See you tomorrow."

CHAPTER TWENTY

After a couple of weeks of relentless backpack runs and drills, Megan showed up to find Jack with nothing - no backpack and no stopwatch.

"You're empty-handed today," she observed. "What does that mean?"

"It means that today we are going to mix things up," he answered in his typical dorky cheerfulness.

"Afraid to get hit by a rock again, are you?"

"No..." Jack stammered. "But you do have remarkably good aim.... But no. Today we are mixing things up by going off-trail."

"Off-trail?" Megan didn't like the sound of that.

"It's just what it sounds like," he answered. "We're getting off the beaten path."

"Why? What for?" Megan wasn't in the mood for another challenge.

"Because it builds mental toughness. If you can run fast off-trail, it makes running a 5k on smooth surfaces that much easier. So follow me."

Megan shrugged her shoulders and followed Jack as he ran down the trail. At least she wasn't lugging that backpack around or running drills. How bad could it be?

A few minutes later Jack stopped at a place where a worn and narrow trail led away from the main trail and weaved through the woods.

"We're going to run on that?" asked Megan.

"If it's good enough for the deer, it's good enough for us," replied Jack.

"I don't know why we are even bothering with this. I'm never going to be as fast as Kristy."

"Forget about Kristy for now," ordered Jack. "Let's just run. Follow me."

Jack ducked under some foliage and disappeared into the woods. Megan shook her head and took off after him following close behind. As the two ran through the forest, they bounded over fallen trees and dodged prickly bushes. Megan had to pay close attention so that any branches that Jack pushed out of his way didn't come swinging back to smack her.

Jack was like a rabbit as he followed the path wherever it led. Megan was having difficulty keeping up. She had to admit it was better than carrying rocks or running drills. But she still had to concentrate and focus on her agility if she wanted to keep pace with Jack while avoiding nature's obstacles. It required fast thinking and quick reflexes on her feet. She had to be fully present in the moment and not get lost in her own head.

After twenty minutes of running, they found themselves deep in the woods. Megan was wholly unfamiliar with her surroundings. She had never been here before. Eventually, the two of them ran up a sloping hillside until they reached a ledge that looked out over a river that was flowing past twenty feet below.

Jack walked right up to the edge and looked over at the water flowing past. He marveled at the view. Megan stood back from the ledge. She was breathing heavily, her heart racing as she watched Jack step closer to the drop-off.

"Wow! Come here and take a look at this!" Jack beckoned. "It's beautiful!"

Megan paused still trying to catch her breath. She could feel the nervous butterflies in her stomach. "No. I'm good," she called out. "I can see from here."

Jack looked puzzled at her words. "No you can't. Don't be silly."

"No. I'm fine right here," she implored.

Jack marched over to Megan and reached out to take her hand. "Come with me. I'll show you."

Megan yanked her hand away. "I said no!"

Jack took a step back at her outburst. Megan bent over and began hyperventilating. She was in the grip of a full-on panic attack.

"Megan, what's wrong?" Jack asked bending down with her to see if she was okay.

"I'm sorry... I'm sorry," was all Megan could muster between shallow breaths.

He put his hand on her back trying to offer some sort of comfort. "About what?"

After a few moments, Megan's breathing began to slow, and she was able to stand up straight. She looked at the forest around her as though searching for words she didn't want to find. Finally, she spoke... words she had not spoken to anyone. "I never told you how my dad died."

Megan took a couple of deep breaths searching for the words. Jack said nothing. For once he was silent. She had his full attention.

At last more words came and Megan began to speak. "Last year, we were hiking up on the bluffs in Hixton Forest in La Crosse - me and my mom and dad."

Again she paused before continuing, speaking almost in a trance-like state. "We were so happy that day - all of us together. But I... I was fooling around on the trail. I kept jumping and clicking my heels together, just being silly, trying to make my dad laugh like I always did - landing with a 'ta da!'"

Megan stopped talking. She couldn't hide the pain in her eyes as they welled up with tears. She wiped them away and pressed on. "But we were on top of the bluff. I kept doing it - not paying attention to how close I was to the ledge. My mom kept telling me to stop and be careful... But I didn't stop... And then I tripped and felt myself going over the ledge."

Megan wiped another tear away. "I would have gone over but for my dad. He saved me. At the last second, he lunged and pushed me back on the trail... but he couldn't keep himself from going over."

Megan stopped talking. Jack stood there frozen in silence as the tears streamed down her face.

Megan spoke again, her voice devoid of any emotion as she stared vacantly ahead. "I remember the screams of my mom. I know I screamed too, but I can't hear myself scream. Don't know why. That plays in my head - over and over. But I never hear my own screams."

Megan looked up at Jack her face etched with tears. "And that is how I killed my dad."

The forest was silent. Neither spoke as they stood staring at each other. The pain on Megan's face betrayed her, revealing the weight she had carried for so long - heavier than any bag of rocks.

Jack's eyes were filled with tears as well. He had no words. Who would? Finally, he spoke. "Megan... Megan, you have to know it was an accident. You are not to blame for your father's death."

Megan wiped another tear, "Well, I would have to disagree with you on that. And I think my mom would as well."

"What?!" Those last words shocked Jack.

"She never says it," Megan answered. "But I know my mom blames me."

Jack shook his head in earnest, "That can't be true."

Megan nodded back in earnest, "Oh, it's true. We never talk about it of course. We never talk about anything anymore. But it's true."

They stood there, two souls lost in the silence and grief. Jack sighed a deep sigh. Then from out of nowhere, he said, "Let's run."

"What?" This was clearly not the response Megan had expected.

"You heard me." And without giving her another moment to think, Jack took off running back the way they came.

"Hey!" yelled Megan shocked by his sudden departure. "Wait up!"

Jack turned back towards Megan. "Catch me!" he yelled.

Megan found herself running through the woods again dodging and ducking obstacles trying her best to keep up with Jack. After several minutes she found herself back on the trail. But there was no Jack. She turned and looked to see him running far down the trail. How rude she thought. He didn't even have the courtesy to wait for her.

She took off after him running hard to catch up. Her legs were driving hard against the trail surface pushing her forward. After a few minutes she caught up to Jack. They continued to run at top speed. Megan could feel herself running through the pain and grief she had been carrying for so long. She ran faster. Now it was Jack's turn to catch up.

They continued the blistering pace as they neared the end of the trail. Megan was pushing her body, mind, and soul past any limit she'd ever experienced - the sadness and melancholy replaced by a fierce determination she had never known.

And then she found another gear. Again Jack had to catch up. Then Jack took the lead. "Stay with me!" he commanded. Megan obeyed. Somewhere in her there was a faster speed and she caught up to Jack. She kept pace with him, barely. She had reached her physical limits, but she kept on. There were just a few more yards to go.

All the way to the end the two raced. Jack finished just a step ahead, and Megan collapsed to the ground in a heap. She lay there on her back gasping for air.

Jack walked over to her and looked down at her. "Are you okay?"

Megan, eyes closed and gasping for breath, could only manage a slight nod yes. She finally opened her eyes to see Jack's outstretched hand in front of her face. She placed her hand in his, again feeling his gentle strength lift her off the ground. He helped her up as they both stood there for a moment still gasping for breath.

"I don't know about you and your mom," said Jack. "And whatever your mom thinks and all that... But I do know one thing for certain."

"What's that?" she asked.

"Kristy is going to have her hands full with you at the 5k."

Finally, Megan smiled.

Jack returned the smile. "Take the weekend off," he said. "Give your body some rest, and we'll meet back here on Monday."

"Aye, aye Captain," she quipped as she stood and saluted.

"What happened to 'yes, sensei'?" he muttered.

"I don't know. Woman's prerogative to change her mind, I guess."

Megan began to walk to her car. "You coming? Actually, I don't even know why I ask. I already know the answer."

"Yes, you do," said Jack. "I'm going to stay and run a bit more."

Megan smiled and shook her head as she continued walking to her car. "I know," she said. "The day I can outrun you..."

"Is the day you'll be ready for the 5k," Jack said finishing her sentence for her.

She opened the car door and looked back at him. "Got it." She hopped in her car and drove off.

———

As Megan pulled out from the road that led to the trail, she didn't notice the car driving past her. It was Kristy.

As Kristy drove past, she looked in her rearview mirror at Megan's car. Her eyes narrowed. She knew that road led to the old running trail. She slowed as she watched Megan's car pull out and drive off in the other direction.

"And just what do you think you're up to, Maggot?" she asked. No one was there to give a response. But no matter. Kristy already surmised the answer to her question.

CHAPTER TWENTY-ONE

For Megan, Saturday was a day of rest and doing nothing. She needed that. She spent a good portion of the day on her bed watching grainy videos of Steve Prefontaine tear across finish lines on her laptop. Over the last several days she could feel herself getting stronger, faster. It lit a curiosity in her to learn more.

She kept to her diet making sure to eat plenty of protein. She endured an icy silence between herself and her mom as she cooked up her own steak for dinner, which she got from Mr. Mahato.

That night she sat on the sofa watching a movie next to her mom who sat in the recliner sipping her wine. It was the closest the two of them could be to enjoying each other's company as no talking was required or expected.

At the end of the movie, Megan got up off the sofa and looked over at her mom and her now empty wine glass.

"I think I am off to bed," said Megan letting a slight yawn escape.

"So soon?"

"Yeah, I'm tired." Megan stretched her arms over her head.

"Need to get my sleep. My body's feeling it after all the workouts."

"Is it really worth it to put yourself through all that just for the 5k?" her mom asked. "I mean, there's no guarantee it will go well even with all the work you are putting in."

Megan could feel the pit in her stomach - the bitter pain of not having those closest to you believe in you. She tried to brush it off. "I know," she answered. "But in a weird way I'm kinda liking the work."

Amy looked down at her empty glass. "Alright. Just remember - I warned you not to get your hopes up."

Megan rolled her eyes. "Don't worry. I won't." She couldn't hide the hurt and disappointment from the sting of her mom's words. "Good night," she snapped, and she stormed off to her bedroom.

Her mom called after her as Megan ran off, "Hey! I'm just saying don't suddenly expect to win is all!"

The bedroom door slammed behind Megan. Amy made her way to the kitchen and poured herself another glass of wine. She took a sip and whispered to herself, "Sheesh. Just trying to help."

———

Late into the night Megan was sound asleep getting the rest her body craved. A beam of light from a full moon shone through the window giving the room an almost magical glow.

Suddenly there was a rap at the window - *BAM BAM BAM!*

Megan stirred, her deep slumber interrupted by the noise. Did she hear something or was it a dream? She couldn't be sure. Then she heard it again. *BAM BAM BAM!*

This time she sat straight up. Someone or something was at the window. Maybe it was a burglar. But burglars didn't usually knock before entering. She jumped out of bed to take a look.

As she made her way to the moonlight, Jack's face appeared in the window. Megan screamed, startled for a moment before recognizing the trespasser. Jack put his finger up to his lips to shush her.

Megan was confused and still not completely awake. "What are you doing here?!" she whispered loudly.

Jack motioned for her to open the window. Megan stepped closer and lifted it open.

"What are you doing here?" she whispered again.

"I've come to get you."

"Get me?"

"Yeah," he answered. "Get your running gear on. I'll wait for you."

"It's the middle of the night," she protested.

"It's a full moon. We'll be able to see perfectly fine."

"I thought you said we weren't training this weekend."

"This isn't training so much as it is an adventure." Jack wasn't taking no for an answer. "Now hurry up."

"Okay. Okay," She whispered realizing the only way to keep from waking her mom was to go with him. "Let a girl get dressed at least."

Jack turned around and waited outside the window while Megan got ready. A few moments later she slid out the window and onto the lawn.

"I can't believe I'm doing this," she remarked.

"You need to live a little," he answered.

"I live a little," she responded defensively.

"Very little. Follow me."

"Hey!" Megan resented Jack judging her life or lack thereof. But there was no time to argue. He was already off and running. Megan caught up and the two ran together down the empty moonlit sidewalk.

As they ran, it was eerie to see the streets all vacant - not another soul around. It was as though they had the entire town to themselves. The city was asleep.

"Where are we going?" she asked.

"Don't worry about that," answered Jack. "Just stay with me."

They followed a winding road that led out of town and into the countryside dotted by farms and forests on either side. A half mile out of town Jack turned off the road and onto an old trail that appeared to go nowhere.

"Where are you taking me?"

"You'll see," was his only response. "Like I said, it's an adventure."

As they ran along the unknown trail, beams of moonlight broke through the forest canopy scattering shadows before them. Megan looked about her trying to see in the darkness of the forest.

"Okay. This is scary." she stammered.

"Naw. This is beautiful," came the cheery response.

"Where are we?"

"This is part of the old Johnson estate," replied Jack.

"Wait. Whose estate?"

"The Charles Johnson estate," Jack explained. "He died a number of years back. His family estate is now in a trust, and no one comes out here."

"Do we have permission to be here?" Megan was now clearly worried.

"I'm sure Mr. Johnson won't mind," said Jack unfazed by her concern for the law.

The two trespassers continued to run through the forest until it opened into a clearing. They ran along the edge of the field, the silence broken only by their footsteps. Jack tapped on Megan's shoulder to get her attention. He pointed and she looked to see what appeared to be three raccoons scurrying to safety just a few yards away.

Megan smiled at the sight of the cuddly critters. The forest at night was a secret world she'd never known. And they had it all to themselves. For the first time in as long as she could remember life felt magical again.

They continued to run across the field through another small group of trees and into another opening in the forest. Megan stopped awestruck by the sight. Jack stopped next to her. Before them was a peaceful lake shimmering like glass with reflections of the night sky dancing on the water's surface.

"Pretty nice, huh?" asked Jack breaking the silence.

Megan stood for a moment taking it all in. "This... this is... beautiful!"

Jack smiled, happy with himself. "I thought you might need a break from the usual routine."

"So what do we do now?" Megan asked.

"Absolutely nothing," answered Jack as he plopped himself down at the base of a large tree and faced the lake. Megan stood there continuing to take in the beauty of the scenery before her. She breathed in the cool midnight air.

She looked down at Jack. He patted the ground next to him, "Have a seat. I won't bite."

Megan plopped herself down next to him. She sat there staring at the glass surface of the lake.

"Hard to believe this is real," she said almost not believing what her eyes could see. "I never even knew there was a lake here."

"Like I said, all this land is in a private trust that never gets used," replied Jack. "It's all been forgotten."

"It's untouched. Completely unblemished. I love it." Megan paused for a moment and then whispered, "Thank you."

"You're welcome," Jack answered softly.

They sat there for several moments enjoying the view and each other's presence in the silence. For Megan it was beautiful. It was perfection.

After several moments, Jack broke the silence again, "And don't worry. I won't ask for a kiss tonight - even though this would be a great opportunity. I won't ruin it for you with that kind of punishment."

Megan smiled and turned to Jack, "Thanks. I appreciate that. And with this view it almost wouldn't feel like punishment."

"Really?" Jack's voice perked up.

"I said almost."

They smiled again at one another and then turned to look at Mother Nature's beauty before them.

"I could spend forever here," sighed Megan "Much better than having to be at home putting up with my mom."

Jack turned to Megan, "You know, you can't hide from your mom."

"Yes, I can. Just watch me."

"I guess I mean, you *shouldn't* hide from her," Jack spoke slowly and intently. "At some point the two of you are going to have to talk about your dad."

"I don't know if I can do that."

There was a long pause before Jack spoke again. "All I know is that avoiding the hard things in life does not make one's life better. Taking the easy way leads to a hard life. But doing what's hard - that's where life's greatest blessings are waiting for us."

Megan stared in wonder at the philosopher next to her - a bit taken aback by his words. "Is that something Prefontaine said?"

"No," said Jack. "But I'm sure he would have agreed with it. It's just how life works."

"I don't understand how someone who dresses as weird as you can be so wise," she teased.

"It's probably the headband," came his matter-of-fact response. "Forces blood to the brain."

Megan chuckled and smiled at Jack's response. She slowly moved her hand closer to Jack's. She took his hand in hers and squeezed it slightly. "Thank you for this," she whispered.

"You're welcome."

Megan leaned into Jack and rested her head on his shoulder. No more words were needed as they sat there enjoying the beauty of the moment together.

CHAPTER TWENTY-TWO

The next few days were the same routine for Megan - lifting weights, working her daily shift, and then running with Jack. In her morning workouts, she was growing stronger and more efficient in her lifts. The bags of canned goods she used when doing squats had grown in number as her increased strength was beginning to show. The hard work was beginning to pay off.

And each little success along the way gave Megan's confidence a much-needed boost. She was beginning to enjoy the work. She certainly liked the improvement she was making.

About a week after her midnight run with Jack, she was again on the floor stacking cans of vegetables onto a display at the end of an aisle. Even the way she stacked cans was quicker and more precise.

Sam Mahato walked up behind Megan as she added cans to the display. "Megan, I need you to deliver some groceries to a couple of customers on your way home. So feel free to leave a little early."

"Sure thing, Mr. Mahato."

"Be sure to use the store's app. And make sure you put in the time the groceries are delivered." Mr. Mahato loved his app.

"Yes, sir," answered an enthusiastic Megan. "Will do."

"Thank you."

Mr. Mahato walked to the back of the store as Megan continued to build an ever higher display of canned vegetables. While placing another can, Megan was startled by the sudden appearance of Kristy on the other side of the display. Next to her stood Gloria and Jennifer.

A tightness gripped Megan's chest. The same old fear crept in, coursing through her veins. But she focused on her breath, taking air in slowly to remain calm. She stepped back from the display to gather herself and put some space between herself and Kristy's entourage.

Kristy stepped closer. "So this is Maggot's hiding place."

Megan tried her best to play cool. "Yep, this is it. Where I hide out every day." She went back to stacking cans.

"Are you running the 5k?" Kristy's question revealed why she was really there.

"I don't know," answered Megan. "Maybe."

"You are, aren't you?" Kristy's jaw tightened as she spoke, "I saw you pulling out from the old running trail at the edge of town. You can't fool me."

"Nope. No fooling you," answered Megan enjoying the anger she stirred in Kristy. "I guess you'll find out for sure on the day of the race."

"You're wasting your time, Maggot." Kristy's attempt to intimidate Megan was falling flat.

Megan cracked an ever-so-slight grin. "You know, I have an aunt who was a teacher and just lost her job. You remind me a lot of her."

"Oh yeah?" Kristy replied. "How so?"

"No class," answered Megan her grin growing wide.

Gloria and Jennifer laughed at the unexpected burn from Megan. Kristy turned and silenced her friends with a glare.

Now it was Kristy's turn to have her blood boil. She looked around for a way to strike back at her foe. She reached over to the display and pulled a can out from the very bottom. The tower of cans tilted and then tumbled over scattering across the floor.

"Oops. Clumsy me," said Kristy as she placed the can on a nearby shelf. "Guess you better get back to work." She turned and began to walk out of the store. "Let's go girls. See you at the 5k, Maggot."

With eyes of steel and a knowing grin on her face, Megan watched her old teammates walk out the door.

Kristy meant to intimidate, but it had the opposite effect. And what was that slight hesitation Megan had noticed in the voice of her nemesis? It certainly wasn't power. No, it was panic.

———

Later that afternoon Megan was running drills with Jack at his post, stopwatch in hand. Megan moved her legs fast. Up down. Up down. Faster and faster. She felt like a machine cruising at a blazing speed.

As she got to Jack, she flew past him in a blur. He hit the button on the stopwatch. For a moment he stared at the device dumbfounded.

Megan turned around and came walking back towards him. "Well Coach?"

"Seriously?" he asked.

"Yeah, seriously. How'd I do?"

Jack held up the stopwatch to Megan so she could see for herself. Her eyes opened wide. Her smile was wider.

"Wow!" she said shocked by the result.

"Yeah. Wow is right."

"Not exactly Prefontaine numbers," she admitted. "But not bad."

"Not bad?" Jack knew his student was being too modest. "That's fast."

"I can get faster." There was a confidence in Megan's voice that wasn't there before.

"What I want to know is how you got that burst of speed."

"Let's just say I ran into Kristy earlier today," Megan admitted.

Jack nodded, now understanding. "Oh. I see.... A little motivation certainly doesn't hurt."

"No," replied Megan. "No. It doesn't."

They smiled at one another. Jack held up his hand and they high-fived celebrating what Megan had just accomplished. The hard work was paying off.

CHAPTER TWENTY-THREE

A few days later Megan found herself in the unusual situation of having a day off from work. She spent much of the day with Riley and Trevor on another round of mini-putt and then a burger at Martin's.

Whenever her friends asked Megan what she had been up to all summer, she just mentioned work and running. But she never mentioned Jack. That was her secret. Not that it mattered if they knew, but she just wanted to keep that part of her life private. It had become something special - something apart from the rest of her life. And she wanted to keep it that way - at least for now.

It was agreed that the mini-putt losers would buy the winner's burger. That got Trevor's attention, and he won in dramatic fashion sinking a thirty foot putt to win by a stroke. As they finished their food, the three friends laughed and joked with one another. For Megan it felt good to reconnect with her friends. And she felt a bit more at ease and comfortable with being herself than she had in a long time.

"What's up with you?" Riley asked.

"What do you mean?" Megan responded, puzzled by the question.

"I mean... I don't know," said Riley trying to find the words. "You just seem more... you, somehow."

"What? I'm always myself." Megan appeared annoyed by Riley pointing out the obvious.

"No, I mean - and don't take this the wrong way." Riley could tell she was digging herself a hole that she might not get out of. "You're not as uptight or on guard as you have been. You seem more - I don't know - free to be yourself."

"Whatever," answered Megan as she blushed feeling suddenly very self-conscious.

"No. She's right." Now Trevor chimed in. "You do seem more at ease than I have seen you in a long time. A real long time."

Megan sighed, "Thank you. It's nice to know I have two psychoanalysts for my best friends."

"Hey, no worries." Riley teased. "That's what we're here for - to get in your mind and figure out what makes you tick. It's what brings joy to our lives."

"Oh, yay," said Megan flatly - no expression on her face.

"Enough of all that," said Riley changing the subject. "I gotta run down to the high school. So I'll see you two later."

"I'll come with," offered Trevor.

"Well... I didn't want to leave Megan by herself," replied Riley.

"What do you mean?" asked Megan. "Why wouldn't I come with to the high school?"

"Well... I just thought that you might not want to go there in case Kristy was there training again."

Megan took a deep breath. "I can handle Kristy."

"You sure?" asked Riley.

"I'll be fine," answered Megan. "Let's go."

The three friends got up out of their booth. Within a few minutes they found themselves walking along the street to the high school. They were coming up to the track where a few track athletes were apparently training with a coach. As they got closer, Megan could see that the athletes were Kristy, Gloria, and

Jennifer. She could also see a man with a stopwatch who appeared to be giving instructions to Kristy.

Almost immediately Gloria and Jennifer came running over to Megan, Riley, and Trevor with just the chain link fence between them.

Gloria looked at Megan. "So, did you come to see what you're up against?"

"Who's the guy with the stopwatch?" asked Megan.

"That is Coach Tom Furnell," replied Gloria.

"Who's he?" asked Riley.

It was Jennifer's turn to chime in. "He just so happens to be one of the best cross country coaches around. He has coached at a number of Big Ten schools."

"What's he doing here?" asked Megan.

"Kristy's dad hired him to coach her for the 5k." Gloria smiled at being the one to give them the news.

Megan's shoulders and chin dropped. She felt deflated as her confidence began to evaporate in the summer heat. "You're kidding me."

"Nope," said Jennifer all excited about the news. "He's one of the best there is. If she can better her time in the 5k, she'll have some of the best schools in the country recruiting her next year. Maybe even Stanford. Her dad says that Coach Furnell is a good investment. Get the best if you want to be the best."

"That's got to cost a pretty penny," said Riley, peering through the fence.

"It is," Jennifer answered. "Not sure how he's affording it, but he is."

"It's all about Stanford," Gloria continued. "Her dad told her if she doesn't drop ten seconds on the 5k she can forget about it. No pressure, right?"

Trevor shook his head, "Yeah, no pressure. Sometimes I'm glad I don't have any natural ability."

Megan turned and began mumbling to herself. "Her own

private coach. And all I've got is a kid stuck in 1976 with no social skills."

"What was that?" asked Gloria.

"Nothing. I was just thinking of something." Megan turned to Trevor and Riley. "Come on guys. Let's go."

The three friends began to walk away.

Jennifer smiled wide and yelled after them, "Good luck with your training!"

As they got further away from the track, Megan turned to her friends. "I don't know how I'm going to compete with that."

"You can do it," said Trevor trying to lift his friend's spirits. "You don't need some over-priced college coach to teach you how to run fast."

"Well, it certainly couldn't hurt," answered Megan.

"Yeah, I suppose not," Trevor admitted.

"You're no help," Riley said to Trevor giving him a slight shove.

Megan continued walking straight ahead with her head down. "This is pointless."

———

Later that afternoon, Megan was once again on the trail with Jack. It was another day of drills with Jack timing Megan's sprints.

Megan's legs pounded the trail as she sprinted towards Jack. As she ran past, he pressed the button on the stopwatch. Jack's brow furrowed as he looked at the time. Megan walked slowly back to her coach. His red headband and long tube socks reminded her that he most definitely was not a Big Ten coach.

"What's up?" he asked.

Jack's words snapped Megan out of her train of thought. "Huh? What?" she asked.

Jack turned the watch and showed it to Megan.

"Oh," was the only response Megan could muster.

"That's all I get? 'Oh'?" Jack was fired up. "How does someone go from lightning fast one day to this the next?"

Megan paced in a circle next to Jack as she stared at the ground. "I don't know."

"You don't know?"

Megan stopped and looked up at Jack. "I saw Kristy again today.... She has a private coach. A *real* college coach to train her for the 5k. Jennifer and Gloria made it sound like she has the race already won. They're probably right."

Jack reached out his hand. "Give me your other shoe?"

"What?" Megan looked confused. "Why?"

"Just give me the shoe," said Jack flatly.

Megan pulled off her shoe and gave it a quick toss in Jack's direction. He grabbed it out of the air, pulled out his Sharpies and started scribbling on the shoe.

"Now what are you writing?" Megan asked, clearly irritated.

"A reminder," answered Jack not looking up from his scribbling.

"Of what?"

"That you're not done yet," answered Jack as he continued scribbling. He continued talking as he marked up her shoe. "It's good that Kristy hired a coach."

"Good? How is that good?" Megan was clearly flustered. "And how can I compete with that?" She hesitated not wanting to hurt Jack's feelings. "No offense."

"None taken. I'm glad she's not going to make it easy." Jack was in earnest as he finished the final touches to her shoe. "If you win, you will have to earn it."

"But I can't win against that," she protested.

Jack tossed the shoe back to Megan. She caught it and looked closely at the markings. This shoe was done up in the same fun and fanciful way as her other shoe. It had the wildflowers and smiley face. But the words running along the bottom were different.

Megan read them aloud, "Go all out." She read aloud, frowning. "Easy for you to say. You're not the one lining up against Kristy and her college coach."

Jack was having none of Megan's feeling-sorry-for-herself attitude. "Believe what you will. Your job is to become the best runner you can be. If you do that, the results don't really matter. But don't go out there knowing you left something on the table. Go all out or not at all. Remember what Steve Prefontaine said. 'To give anything less than your best is to sacrifice the gift.'"

"I'm not really in the mood for Prefontaine right now!" Megan shot back.

Jack huffed, "It's not just Prefon - You know what. It doesn't matter. Let's cut it short today. Go home. Get out of your head, and let's start again tomorrow."

"Fine," Megan replied, "Whatever." She began to march off to her car when she turned back. "You say shoes are about the future, about where we're going. But what about your shoes? They're stuck in 1978. Maybe *you're* the one who's not moving forward, not going all out."

Jack stood there as the two glared at one another. Neither said a word. Megan finally threw up her arms in exasperation and turned and walked away.

She started the car, paused with her hands on the wheel, and glanced back at the trail. She watched as Jack turned and ran off in the opposite direction, past the trees, and out of sight. Megan tightened her grip, exhaled, and drove away in silence, her frustration and anger ready to boil over.

CHAPTER TWENTY-FOUR

Megan stomped through the front door slamming it behind her. The drive home did nothing to improve her mood.

The slam of the door startled her mom seated on the sofa with a glass of wine. "Hey!" she yelled. "Don't slam the door!" Amy readjusted herself on the sofa, careful not to spill her wine. "And what are you doing home so soon? I thought you'd still be running."

"Cut it short today," replied a curt Megan as she walked into her bedroom.

Amy stood up and stumbled for a moment as she made her way to the kitchen spilling her wine in the process. "Dammit!" She grabbed some paper towels and began to wipe up the red liquid splashed on the island counter.

Megan walked quickly out of her bedroom straight to the kitchen and opened the fridge.

"I got some leftover fried rice in there if you want some," Amy offered as she finished cleaning up her spilled drink.

"No thanks. I'll just take a protein shake," answered Megan scanning the fridge.

"I know. My food's not good enough for you," her mom grumbled.

Megan grabbed the fried rice from the fridge. "Fine! I'll eat the frickin' fried rice!"

Amy turned to face her daughter with the wine soaked paper towels still in her hand. "Watch your tone, young lady!" She wasn't in the mood for any back talk.

Megan shoved the rice into the microwave, slammed the door, and hit reheat. Amy walked over to the garbage bin to throw out the paper towels. When she opened it, the garbage was full and overflowing.

Amy threw up her hands, exasperated. "How many times do I have to ask you to take out the garbage before you do it?!"

"What?!" Megan bit back. "I just got home! I would have gotten to it."

"You never listed to me," her mom groused shaking her head slightly.

"What's the big deal?" Megan turned to her mom and stared directly at her. "It's just garbage!"

Amy closed her eyes with clenched fist as she kept repeating "You never listen to me. You never listen to me. You never listen to me."

"Why?!" Megan barked interrupting her mom. She stepped closer. "Why does it matter?!"

Amy continued to repeat those same words louder and louder as her eyes closed tighter and her fists clenched harder. "You never listen to me! You never listen to me!"

Megan exploded, "It's just garbage! Why does it matter?!"

Amy opened her eyes and screamed at her daughter just inches from her face, "Because your dad would still be alive if you had just listened to me!!"

Megan stepped back in horror, her mom's words piercing her like a dagger to the heart.

Amy recoiled, shocked by her own words. The look on her face. If only she could snatch the words out of the air and take them back. But it was too late. Her words had escaped her in a fit of rage. Only a blanket of brutal silence remained to smother the two women.

Finally, Amy spoke trembling, "Meggie... I'm - I'm sorry.... I... I didn't mean that. I..." She took a step towards her daughter extending her hand.

Megan backed up into the stove. She dodged out of the way to avoid her mother's reach. "Don't touch me," she cried with a bitter pain in her voice and tears welling up in her eyes.

Amy fought back her own tears as she pleaded with her daughter, "Megan, please. I didn't mean to -" She again stepped towards Megan with an outstretched hand.

Megan dodged her a second time. "Yes, you did."

"No, I just..."

Tears streamed down Megan's cheeks. "You've always blamed me for Dad's death. So do I. I know I'm to blame."

"No. No, that's not true," her mom answered shaking her head. "It was an accident."

Megan shook her head in response. "No. You finally said how you really feel. You blame me. And why shouldn't you? It was my fault."

Amy stepped back and put her hand over her heart as though the words had caused her physical pain. She gasped, "Megan."

The two stood there staring at each other both in tears. For a long moment no words were spoken. And then *BEEP BEEP BEEP*. The silence was broken by the timer on the microwave.

Megan bolted for the front door.

"Megan wait!" her mom cried out.

But Megan didn't wait. She didn't stop. She ran out the front door slamming it behind her.

Amy stood there frozen unable to move. "Megan!" She yelled. But it was no use. Megan was gone.

CHAPTER TWENTY-FIVE

Megan's car skidded to a stop. She jumped out and ran up onto the trail.

"Jack!" she called out. "Jack!"

From down the trail he came running towards her. Jack rushed to Megan taking both her hands in his. "What's wrong?" He asked looking intently at Megan and the pain in her eyes.

"My mom..." Megan cried barely able to get the words out.

"What about your mom?"

Megan fought through the tears trying to speak. "She said... she said it was my fault that my dad died."

"What?!" Jack was taken aback, shocked by Megan's words.

Megan nodded tears falling, "She said... if I had just listened to her... my dad would still be alive."

Jack pulled her into his arms, whispering, "Oh, Megan."

Megan sobbed, her head on Jack's chest. After a moment she continued, "She's felt that way this whole time. And she finally said it." Megan looked up into Jack's eyes. "And you know what? She's right."

Jack shook his head, "No."

Megan nodded, "Yes. It's my fault. If I had just listened to her, my dad would be alive today."

"Megan, stop," Jack protested. "Your dad would never want you to think like that."

"Well, it's true."

"No," Jack continued. "You were just being your fun, silly self."

"No. I wouldn't listen," answered Megan still shaking her head.

"Because you're a teenager," said Jack still holding her in his arms. "You can't see the risks like adults can.... It was an accident."

Megan buried her face in Jack's chest and sobbed, "My fault."

Jack held Megan back just far enough from him so he could lift her chin with his hand to look her in the eyes. "No. And you want to know something else? Any loving father would gladly give his life to save the life of his child. Your dad gave his life to save you. And he would make that same decision every time. Because that is how much he loved you... and still does."

Megan wiped her eyes. "I wish I could tell him how much I love him."

"You have to believe that he knows. I believe that with all my heart. You need to believe it too."

They put their arms around each other as Megan rested her head against Jack's chest. He gently caressed her hair as she continued to weep softly in his arms.

Jack went on, "And you know what else?"

"What?" asked Megan looking up into his eyes.

"Your mom loves you too."

"She hates me."

"No."

"Yes."

Jack met her eyes. "You need to go back and talk to her," he insisted.

"I can't." Megan looked terrified at the prospect of facing her mom. "I don't want to go back there."

"Megan." Jack's voice was soft but stern.

"Can't I just stay here... with you?" she whispered. "And I won't say anything mean about your shoes. I love your shoes. I'm sorry about what I said. It wasn't fair."

Jack sighed and held Megan tight as she again rested her head on his chest. "It's okay. And I'm glad you like my shoes." He paused for a moment then gently lifted her chin to look her in the eye. "Now what do you want to do?" he asked.

Megan took a deep breath and paused for a moment. She looked up at Jack. "Let's run."

"You sure?" He wasn't expecting that answer.

"I'm sure," she said. "Let's go!"

Megan stepped back, wiped her eyes, and raced down the trail. Jack caught up to her and together they set a brisk pace. They turned to look at each other. That steely determination again filled Megan's eyes. Then they both smiled at each other knowing what to do. In another instant both Megan and Jack kicked their pace into overdrive as they sped off down the trail.

———

It was late, and Amy was sound asleep on the couch when Megan finally returned home. The front door opened slowly as she crept in and quietly closed the door behind her. She tiptoed past her mom and into her bedroom.

Amy awoke to the sound of the bedroom door closing. She slowly got up and looked out the front window to see Megan's car parked in the driveway. She sighed a sigh of relief as she placed her hand over her heart.

She walked over to Megan's bedroom door and gently knocked. "Megan," she whispered. There was no answer. She knocked again. "Megan, can we talk?"

"I'm tired, Mom," came the muted voice from inside the room. "Just going to bed."

"Okay," replied Amy. "Goodnight."

"Goodnight," came the muffled reply.

Amy walked slowly back to the couch. She picked up her half-full glass of wine. She lifted it about to take a sip. But she stopped with the glass just inches from her mouth. She stared at the wine, then slowly set it back down on the end table.

She turned off the living room light and went to bed. The wine glass sat untouched in the darkness.

CHAPTER TWENTY-SIX

Over the next couple of weeks, Megan stuck to her usual routine while doing her best to avoid her mom. Whenever Amy wanted to talk, Megan had no time and was headed out the door. It had worked so far, but Megan knew she couldn't keep that up.

One day she found herself at work placing magazines in the display rack. She was flipping through a runner's magazine when she was startled to see Riley peeking at her from over the top of the rack.

"My gosh!" exclaimed Megan catching her breath. "You scared me!"

Riley walked around the rack to where Megan was. "Sorry about that. Just wondering where you've been hiding. Haven't seen you around for the last few weeks."

"Yeah. Sorry about that," replied Megan. "Just been busy working and training for the 5k."

"How's that going?"

"It's been... fun," Megan answered trying her best to hold back a smile.

"Glad to hear it. And how's your mom?"

Megan gave her friend a hard stare and shook her head. "Don't ask."

Riley put up her hands and took a step back. "Okay then. Let's not go there." She tried to change the subject. "Trevor's been asking where you've been."

"Yeah..." Megan responded in a flat monotone voice. "I don't think that's going to happen."

"Yeah, I know. You know him too well. Whatever."

"No, it's not that," said Megan.

"Well, what is it then?" her friend asked.

Megan paused, biting her lip. Should she say it or not? She had kept Jack a secret for so long. She finally blurted it out, "I met someone, okay?"

"You met someone?!" Riley was genuinely shocked.

Megan glanced around to see if anyone heard. "Shhhh," she said with her finger to her lips to keep Riley quiet.

"Sorry," Riley whispered. "You met someone? Who? Is it someone who works here?

"No. It's no one you know," answered Megan as she placed another magazine in the rack.

"Who is it?" Riley begged to know.

Megan stopped putting magazines in the rack and stared intently at her friend. "It's some guy I met while running on the trail outside of town."

"Some random guy you met on the trail?" To Riley this was sounding more than a little odd.

"Yes," Megan attempted to explain. "His name is Jack. He's not from around here. He's in town for the summer visiting his mom. We run together and he's been helping me train for the 5k."

Riley grinned a big knowing grin. "No wonder you've been spending so much time *training*."

"No. It's not like that," Megan insisted. "At least not yet."

"How serious is it?"

"I don't know."

"Have you kissed?"

Megan blushed at the question. "No. But he's asked."

"And you turned him down?" asked a clearly perplexed Riley.

"It's hard to explain," replied Megan.

Riley looked up at nothing in particular as she thought out loud, "So you've rejected his advances." She paused and looked back at Megan. "You ever going to make a move?"

"I was thinking of taking the relationship off trail," admitted Megan. "Maybe ask him out for a burger and a movie."

"Well, you better move," insisted Riley. "Summer's coming to an end. And I want to meet this Jack."

"You will. I just -"

Mr. Mahato walked up to the girls interrupting their conversation. "Megan, I have a delivery for you to make on your way home. You can leave now and go home a bit early if you would like."

"Thank you, Mr. Mahato," answered Megan. "I'll go right now."

"Very good," he nodded. "Have a good night."

"You too."

As Mr. Mahato walked away, Megan turned to Riley. "Sorry, I have to go." She grabbed the remaining magazines still in the box and started to rush off.

Riley called out to her friend, "We are definitely finishing this conversation at a later date."

Megan waved back to Riley. "Okay, okay. Later."

After putting the box of magazines away, Megan headed to the front of the store where the groceries to be delivered were waiting. She glanced at the address card taped to the box. It read, "Joanne Scissors, 332 Sunset Lane."

"Huh," Megan said to herself. "Jack's mom. Can't be more than one Scissors in town."

She picked up the box of groceries and headed out the door.

CHAPTER TWENTY-SEVEN

Megan drove across town looking down occasionally at the map on her phone. As she got close to her destination, the neighborhood was much like her own.

She finally got to the house and pulled into the driveway. The house was a nondescript ranch, almost identical to hers. Megan got out of her car and walked up to the door with the box of groceries in hand.

She was excited to finally meet Jack's mom, and maybe even Jack would be there if he wasn't already at the trail. But knowing Jack he was probably already at the trail waiting for Megan to get done with work.

She rang the doorbell and stood there shifting her weight from one foot to the other waiting in nervous anticipation for the door to open. She was about to ring the bell again when she heard the door unlock from the inside.

As the door slowly opened, Megan peered around the door to get a first look at Jack's mom. As the door fully opened, an old woman in her mid-eighties, short, with gray hair, and bifocals stood there looking up at her.

Megan furrowed her brow, confused. "Mrs. Scissors?" she asked.

"Yes," replied the old woman. "You must have my groceries."

"Ah... yes. Yes, I do," answered Megan still unsure about just who she was talking to.

"Can you bring them in for me and set them on the counter?" asked the woman. "I'm getting too old to carry such heavy things."

"Um... sure," answered Megan. She walked in following the old woman to the kitchen where she placed the box on the counter. "You're Mrs. Scissors?" she asked again. "Mrs. Joanne Scissors?"

"Yes, that's me. That's my name."

Megan tilted her head. "Are you Jack's grandma?"

"Excuse me?" Joanne Scissors looked at Megan as though she didn't hear the question.

Megan asked again, "Are you Jack Scissors's grandma?"

"Oh, heavens no dear," she chuckled. "I'm Jack's mom. Both his grandmas died many years ago."

Megan's look of bewilderment only grew. None of this made any sense. "I'm sorry. Did you say you're Jack's mom?"

"Yes, that's me, Jack Scissors' mom." Joanne picked a can of vegetables out of the box and turned back to Megan who stood there with a look of consternation about her face. Joanne continued, "You must have seen his memorial plaque in the trophy case at school."

"I'm sorry. What?" Megan's brain couldn't make sense of the words she was hearing.

"The memorial plaque," Joanne answered. "I didn't think kids these days still took the time to look at all that. It's nice to know that some of you do. Jack would have liked that."

"I'm sorry," replied Megan apologizing again. "What do you mean by 'Jack would have liked that'?"

Joanne sighed as she appeared lost in thought for a moment. "I think he would like to know that some of the kids still remember him this many years after his death."

Megan staggered back, catching herself on the refrigerator door.

"You okay, dear?" Joanne asked taking a step towards Megan.

Megan tried to retreat but the fridge wasn't about to budge. "Yeah. Yeah. I'm fine," she insisted.

"You don't look fine. Here let me get you some water." Joanne Scissors turned to the sink to pour a glass for the troubled girl.

Megan began to sidestep and slide her way out of the kitchen and towards the front door. "No. I'm sorry. Really. I just... I have to go."

Megan bolted for the door leaving Joanne Scissors there stunned by her abrupt departure. She ran to her car, jumped in, and backed out of the driveway. As she sped off, Joanne Scissors stood in the doorway as she waved and said, "Thanks for the groceries!"

———

Megan weaved in and out of traffic as she frantically sped across town. "No. No, this can't be," she said to herself. "It can't be."

She sat forward in her seat darting her head about as she waited behind another car at a red light. As the light turned green, Megan swerved into the next lane, narrowly cutting off another car. It honked its horn at Megan. She didn't care. She had to get to the high school.

A couple minutes later she pulled into the high school parking lot, her tires squealing as she turned the corner. She parked askew outside the yellow lines. No matter. She jumped out of her car and ran to the front doors. She tried a door. Locked. She tried another. It opened, and she dashed inside.

Megan ran down the main hall to where the trophy case was. She made a hard stop and pressed her hands against the glass. She scanned the display of trophies and plaques highlighting the star athletes from years past.

She scanned through the 90s, then the 80s. "Where are you?" she asked as the tension she felt throughout her body grew stronger. "Where are you?"

She reached the 70s and continued searching as she got near the bottom of the case. Then she suddenly stopped cold. She stared as though in a daze, unable to move.

There, in the bottom corner of the trophy case, partially covered by other trophies, was a dust-covered plaque. On the plaque Megan could see a picture of a tall, lanky kid wearing a red head band, long tube socks, short shorts, and a Steve Prefontaine t-shirt.

Megan read the words inscribed on the plaque. "In memory of Jack Scissors 1961-1978. 1977 All Conference Track and Field."

Megan caressed the glass with her hand as tears welled up in her eyes. A single tear slid down her cheek. "Jack... my Jack," she whispered as another tear fell. "You're not real."

CHAPTER TWENTY-EIGHT

Megan raced to the trail in a daze, shocked by her discovery. None of it made sense. Had the boy she spent the whole summer with even been real? She had felt his arms around her, knew the gentle strength of his touch. He had to be real. Didn't he?

As she pulled up to the trail, her tires skidded to a stop. She jumped out of the car. She hesitated. Did she even want to know? She started again for the trail. She had to know.

Megan stepped onto the trail with delicate steps as though stepping onto the first frozen ice of winter. She called out, "Jack!" She turned and looked down the trail in one direction, then turned and looked the other way.

She called out again, "Jack!" She turned around. Still nothing. "Jack!" she yelled as she turned in a circle. "I know you're -"

She turned again and there he was - standing only thirty feet from her on the trail wearing those same 70s clothes he had worn every day prior.

"I'm here," he said in a measured, reserved tone.

Megan began to walk slowly towards Jack. "I met your mom today," she said doing her best to remain calm.

"I know."

She stepped closer. "I went to the high school."

"I know. I..."

Megan cut him off as she took another step closer. "I saw your picture in the trophy case."

Jack said nothing as she continued to walk slowly towards him. She finally stopped just inches from him. Her breathing was slow and heavy as she tried to remain calm. Megan raised her hand, stuck out her index finger and gently poked Jack in the chest. He certainly felt real.

"Are you really here?" she asked.

"I'm really here," he answered.

Megan took a step back. "But are you real?"

"I'm real," he replied. "I'm just no longer real... the way you're real."

"Can anyone else see you?"

"No. Just you."

"That's why you never leave the trail," she said beginning to put it all together. "Well, except for our midnight run... when no one else was around."

Megan turned in the opposite direction away from Jack. She was lost in a swirl of thoughts and emotions trying to make sense of it all. She turned back to him, "Why are you here?"

"I came to help you... and your mom."

"Really?" Megan's eyes grew wide, shocked by Jack's words. "Well, since you have been here, things with my mom have only gotten worse. At least before you came we were actually talking to each other."

"No," he replied. "You had to have the courage to face her."

"Well, I did, and look where it got me."

"Megan, it's not like that." Jack was in earnest now... and so was Megan.

"I guess I should be grateful. God sent me an angel, ghost, or whatever you are, to help me...." Megan fought back tears. She whispered, "I just don't think you helped."

She turned, lost in her thoughts, and took a few more steps

away from Jack. She stopped and turned back to the boy with a puzzled look on her face.

"Something I don't understand," she said. "Since you knew that you are not real in the same way I'm real... why did you let me lo-" Megan caught herself and started again, "Why did you let me *like* you?"

"I'm sorry." Jack answered, his voice humble and contrite. "I didn't mean for us to - "

Megan cut him off, "Yes. Yes, you did... How many times did you ask for a kiss?"

"I can explain -"

Megan didn't want to hear it. "Taking me for a run to the lake at midnight." Her eyes filled with tears and they began to slide down her face. "Letting me pour my heart out to you."

"I'm sorry. I just -"

"All that..." She stopped and looked down at the ground lost in thought again. She looked up at him and wiped the tears from her face. "And now I can't even ask you out for a burger and a movie," she said, barely able to get the words out.

Megan could feel the blood rushing to her face. Embarrassed by her own emotions, she turned away again to wipe her eyes. She turned back to Jack as she tried to speak through the tears, "You were the only person I could talk to... and you're not real."

"Megan, please!" Jack's eyes began to well up with tears as he reached his hand out to her.

Megan stepped away from him shaking her head. "No... No, I don't think it's a good thing to keep seeing you when I can't... see you."

"Megan," Jack pleaded. "You can still see me."

She continued to walk backwards putting more distance between them. "You know what I mean." She wiped more tears away.

Jack held out his hand again. A desperate whisper was all he could utter, "Megan."

"No. I'm sorry," she replied, her voice turning to resignation. "I can't... I can't do this."

Megan turned and ran to her car.

Jack yelled out to her, "Megan, please!"

But Megan kept running. She didn't stop. She didn't dare look back.

CHAPTER TWENTY-NINE

Amy Zane stood in the kitchen chopping vegetables at the island counter while watching the TV play in the living room. The front door flew open as Megan ran into the house.

The sudden noise startled Amy, and she nearly cut herself. She pulled the knife away from her fingers as she watched her daughter run past her in tears. Megan ran straight to her bedroom slamming the door behind her.

Amy walked over to the bedroom door and knocked. "Megan? Is everything okay?... Megan?"

There was no response. She put her ear closer to the door and heard the muffled sound of crying.

"Megan. What's wrong?" There was no response. "Megan, please!" Amy pleaded.

"Nothing's wrong," came a tearful voice from inside the bedroom. "Just leave me alone."

"Honey, I'm making dinner. I think you'll like it. Lots of protein."

All Amy could hear was more crying. Megan again spoke up through the tears, "Please just go away. I'm not hungry. Really. I just want to be left alone."

Amy sighed. Nothing she said would make her daughter

come out of her room. "Okay, dear," she answered, trying to conceal her worry. "I'll be here if you need anything."

Amy walked back to the kitchen. She looked back at the bedroom door, a look of distress etched on her face. She went back to slowly chopping the vegetables hoping in vain that Megan would eventually come out and tell her what was wrong.

————

Megan sat on her bed rocking back and forth holding a pillow tightly in her arms as she sobbed quietly, trying not to let her mom hear. Between sobs she would cry out in a desperate whisper, "Dad... why? Why, Dad?"

She continued to sob. "Was this the answer to my prayer? No... it can't be. It can't. God wouldn't be that cruel.... Would he?"

She pressed the pillow against her face, trying to muffle the sound of her sobs. "Dad, help me. Please help me." It was all she could say, over and over, until she finally tired, closed her eyes, and fell asleep.

————

Early the next morning Megan's mom stepped out of her bedroom in her nightgown still rubbing sleep from her eyes. She walked down the hall towards the kitchen and stopped at the closed door of Megan's bedroom.

She raised her hand to knock, then stopped. She went into the kitchen and started to brew a pot of coffee. She went back and stood outside the door to Megan's bedroom. Amy knocked gently on the door.

"Come on, sleepy head," she said. "Wake up and let's talk."

Amy waited and listened by the door. Nothing. She walked back to the kitchen, pulled out a couple slices of bread, and placed them in the toaster. She walked back to Megan's bedroom door. This time she knocked louder.

"Come on Megan! You can't hide all day!"

She listened for a moment. No answer. She tried to turn the handle. To her surprise it wasn't locked. She turned the handle and slowly nudged the door open expecting to see the usual lump under the covers.

"Megan?" Amy asked as she slid the door open. She stepped in and looked about the room. It was empty.

"Megan?" she called out again.

Amy's heart pounded as she searched the room - under the bed, in the closet, behind the door. Nothing. She ran out of the bedroom and opened the front door. Megan's car was still parked in the driveway. Amy turned back around and stood in the living room not knowing what to do.

She cried out, her voice rising in panic, "Megan!"

CHAPTER THIRTY

Amy rushed into Mahato's Grocery Store, stopped, and scanned the people around her. She spotted the girl at checkout and asked her where to find Mr. Mahato. The girl directed her to the back of the store.

Amy pushed through the swinging doors to the back of the store. She found Sam Mahato seated at his desk.

"Sam, have you seen Megan this morning?"

Sam looked up from his paperwork. "Amy!" His voice was upbeat and friendly. "So good to see you. Ah, no I have not seen Megan this morning. First time she's been late. I was just about to call her. Is everything okay?"

"No. Everything is not okay. She's missing!"

"What?!" Sam stood up. Amy had his full attention.

"She came home last night crying and wouldn't come out of her room. I woke up this morning and she's gone. But her car is still in the driveway. I can't find her anywhere."

"Have you called the police?"

"No... It's just that... I mean... we had an argument a few nights ago and... she's hardly said a word to me since. I just need to find her. Can you help me?"

"I'll certainly help in any way I can," Sam offered. He paused for a moment thinking. "She seemed fine when she left here yesterday. She had a delivery on her way home, but she never checked in on our app to confirm she delivered the groceries. She's usually very good about doing that."

Amy put her head back and closed her eyes exasperated, "I don't know where to look. And I know police will tell me it hasn't been long enough for them to start to look for her. I don't know what to do." Worry and fear were etched across her face.

Sam thought some more. "Wait. I know." He reached into his pocket and grabbed his phone. "I don't know why I didn't think of this first."

"What's that?" Amy asked, desperate for anything to give her hope.

Sam looked at his phone pressing a few buttons on the screen. "My app allows me to track my employees who also have my app on their phone. I just use it to make sure they come straight back from making deliveries, so they're not wasting time." He pressed a few more buttons. "Hold on... there!"

"What?" asked Amy.

"I found her... I think. But what is she doing way out there?"

"Where?"

Sam turned the phone to show the map with Megan's location to Amy.

"I don't even know where that is," said Amy, confused at what the app was indicating for Megan's location. "It's a long way from the nearest road. Can I use your phone to go get her?"

"She probably just had to get away for a while," said Sam trying to calm Amy. "I tell you what, since she doesn't seem to want to talk to you right now, let me go get her."

"No. I should be the one," Amy protested.

"Let me go find her," he offered. "Go home, and I will get her and bring her to you. I think she might talk to me. If I have any trouble, I will call you right away."

Amy shook her head no. "I just feel like if I don't get her, I'll be an even worse mom than I already am." Tears began to well up in her eyes. "You don't know what I said. I…"

Sam raised his hand. "Amy," he said gently. "I got this. Let me go get her, okay?"

Amy broke down crying. She nodded, "I'm sorry… You're right. Just bring her home to me."

Sam put his arm around Amy and handed her a tissue for her to wipe her eyes and nose. "Go home," he said. "I'm sure I'll be back with her shortly."

Amy wiped her tears, nodded to Sam, and slowly walked out the door to go home.

Sam looked down at his phone again. His eyes widened as he realized where the pin was. "That's the old Johnson estate!" The realization caught him off guard. "Megan Zane, how did you get way out there?"

CHAPTER THIRTY-ONE

A short time later, Sam Mahato found himself driving slowly along a lonely county road just a mile out of town. As he drove along, he was looking for something along the side of the road. It had been a long time since he had been out this way.

He puttered along until he saw something familiar. He stopped his car and took a closer look. There, in the woods he spotted it - a thinly worn trail. *That's it!* He thought to himself.

Sam parked his car on the side of the road and ducked under some overhanging branches to follow the trail. He followed the path through the undergrowth deep into the woods. He checked the map on his phone as he neared the pin marking Megan's location.

After several minutes, he came to a clearing with a beautiful meadow. He walked past the meadow and to another patch of woods. As he stepped out of the last patch of trees, a beautiful lake came into view. It was all just as he had last seen it.

The map on his phone indicated that he was very close to his target. He looked around and there off to his right he spied someone sitting up against a large tree facing the lake. It was Megan.

Megan sat there in the quiet of the morning staring blankly at the beautiful landscape before her. The sound of footsteps getting closer interrupted the silence. She could sense the presence of someone casting a shadow over her.

Megan looked up. Sam Mahato stood beside her. She turned back to the lake. "How'd you find me?" she asked flatly.

Sam held up his phone with a proud smile on his face. "The new and improved Mahato Grocery App." There was no reaction from his audience. "Mind if I sit down," he asked.

"Free country," she muttered.

Sam sat down next to Megan and stretched out his legs. "That is a long walk. My legs are not as young as they used to be." He looked out over the lake. "Beautiful spot. How did you find this place?"

"Someone brought me here once."

"Anyone I know?"

"No," Megan answered. "Just somebody that I used to know. It doesn't matter now."

Sam turned to Megan. "Your mother is worried sick about you."

Megan scoffed, still staring at the lake. "My mom - worried sick about me." She finally turned to Sam. "She blames me for my dad's death. Told me it was my fault. Did she tell you that?"

Sam let out a deep sigh. "She told me she said something very hurtful to you," he said. "I know she is very sorry."

Megan turned back to the lake. "Some things can't be undone. Some words can't be unsaid."

Sam thought for a few moments. "Megan, in life it is always the ones that we love the most that will cause us the most pain. Not because they mean to, but because they are human. You cannot expect anyone, not even a parent, to be perfect. We all make mistakes."

"You don't," she argued.

"Ha!" He chuckled. "Now it's my turn to laugh. You would not think so well of me if you had known me in the couple of years after my Lana passed away."

"You were married?"

"Mmm hmm."

"I never knew that."

"Well, it's not something I usually talk about," he answered. "Especially with employees."

Megan looked at Sam. "How did she die?"

"Cancer. My two boys were about your age at the time." Sam looked down and picked a handful of grass from the ground. He rolled the grass around in his hands as he spoke. "I am ashamed to admit that I was not the best father to them after she passed. I shut myself off from the world... and my boys. Much like your mom has."

"But you weren't to blame for your wife's death," said Megan as she looked intently at Sam.

"No. And you weren't responsible for your dad's death. And if your dad could talk to you, he would tell you the same thing."

Tears welled up in Megan's eyes. "I lose everyone I love. My dad, now my mom... and Jack."

"Whose Jack?" asked Sam.

"Nothing," Megan said quickly turning back to the lake. "He's nobody. Really."

"Well, I don't know about this Jack. But I do know that you are loved by your mom and she needs your forgiveness." Sam paused for a moment and then said, "And you need to forgive her."

"Why?" asked an incredulous Megan. "Why do I need to forgive her?"

"Because we forgive," Sam said softly, deliberately. "Especially those we love. We must, otherwise there would be no one to love. And that would be a pretty bleak world."

Megan sighed, "Why does this have to be so hard?"

"I don't know," said Sam. "I only know that doing what's

hard, well, that's where life's greatest blessings are waiting for us."

Megan stared intently at Sam, a curious look on her face. "Who told you to say that?"

Sam looked confused by the question. "No one."

"No really," Megan implored. "Where did you hear that?"

"It doesn't matter. I just know it's true." Sam sat there quietly for a moment staring at the lake. "If there is ever a sad moment in heaven it will be when we get there and we get to see all the blessings God had in store for us but we rejected them because we thought they were too hard." He turned to Megan. "I think you are at one of those moments with your mom."

"Maybe," answered Megan. "What you said about doing what's hard is where life's blessings are waiting for us - someone told me the same thing recently."

"Well, if you must know," said Sam. "I heard it from an old friend of mine from high school. We used to run out here together each of us pushing the other to run faster." Sam paused for a moment. "He died long ago. But he was the one who used to tell me that."

Megan stared at Sam engrossed in his words. "His name. What was his name?"

"He was another Jack," he answered. "You've met his mom. You delivered groceries to her yesterday. Joanne Scissors."

Megan gasped holding her hand to her heart.

"Is everything okay?" asked Sam.

Megan quickly stood up. She took a deep breath as she took a long look out over the natural beauty before her.

So many thoughts raced through her mind. Memories of all that had taken place that summer flashed before her. She could suddenly see it all in a different light – from a higher perspective. So much had happened. She was no longer the same person she had been less than three months ago. She had grown so much. Until now she hadn't realized just how much.

She thought about the prayers she had whispered – to her

dad, to God. So many prayers that she thought went unheard and unanswered. But they had indeed been heard and answered. Maybe not in the way she wanted. But they were answered in the way she needed them to be answered. In ways that forced her to grow and become more.

She smiled as she took it all in, realizing that everything that had happened led her here to this moment. She was right where she should be.

Megan looked down at Sam who was still waiting for an answer to his question. "Yes," she answered. "Everything is okay. In fact, everything is perfect."

She turned to look out over the lake and trees beyond. Finally, she turned back to Sam. "Mr. Mahato, can you please take me home?"

Sam stood up and smiled. "I'd be happy to."

CHAPTER THIRTY-TWO

Amy paced nervously back and forth in the kitchen. She didn't know what to do with herself as she waited for word from Sam.

Out of habit, she opened the fridge and grabbed a half-full bottle of wine. She opened it and was about to pour herself a glass. Pausing for a long moment, she stared at the bottle. "No more," she whispered, setting the glass down.

Amy walked over to the kitchen sink and poured the rest of the wine down the drain. Setting the empty bottle on the counter, she went back to the fridge and pulled out two more bottles of wine. She opened another and started pouring it into the sink when the front door opened. It was Megan.

Amy looked up. For a long moment, the two women stared at one another, tears in their eyes, the silence broken only by the sound of the wine that continued to pour down the drain.

Megan shut the door and ran to her mom. Amy set the bottle down and ran around the counter to meet her daughter. The two embraced. Amy wrapped her daughter in her arms squeezing her tight.

"I'm so sorry," said Amy through tears that began to slide down her cheeks.

"I'm sorry too," replied Megan also in tears.

"Please forgive me," Amy pleaded. "I never should have said that. I -"

Megan interrupted and looked up at her mom, "No. It's okay. I should have listened to you."

Amy took Megan's face in her hands. "No. It's not your fault. Never was. It was just an accident."

"I know. I know," said Megan crying.

Amy sniffled and wiped her tears. "I love you more than anything in the world. I'm sorry the way I've been."

"It's alright."

"No.... No....," Amy answered. "I'm going to get some help.... I know I need someone to talk through everything I've kept bottled up. And I've taken it all out on you. I'm so sorry."

They hugged each other again, tightly holding on to each other through the tears.

"I love you, Mom," Megan whispered.

"I love you too, Meggie," whispered Amy.

———

The sun was still high in the sky as Megan stepped out onto the running trail. She breathed in deeply the fresh summer air.

She looked up at a few clouds slowly floating past - behind them a deep blue sky. It had been too long since she had taken the time to notice such things - the beauty of the world all around her.

She stretched, then looked in both directions. Not a soul in sight. She waited for a few moments, then finally called his name. "Jack!" she shouted. She looked around, but there was no answer.

She called out again, "Jack!" Again she waited. Nothing.

Megan frowned, disappointed by the silence. She couldn't wait all day. It was time to run. And so she took off down the trail. For the first time in a long time she ran alone.

After several minutes of running at a good pace, she arrived at the point in the trail where the narrow path began that took her and Jack to the ledge overlooking the stream. She paused for a moment, pondering which path to take. She remembered Jack's words as they played in her head, *Doing what's hard - that's where life's greatest blessings are waiting for us.*

Without another moment's hesitation she ducked into the foliage and headed down the narrow path. She ran a fast pace as she dodged and ducked her way through nature's obstacle course. She was light on her feet as she bounded down the path.

A smile appeared on her face as she realized that she could have never done this at the beginning of the summer. She began to smile and even laugh as she continued on the adventure.

Within a few minutes Megan arrived at the ledge overlooking the river. Again she stopped about thirty feet from the drop off. She took a few deep breaths, then took several deliberate steps towards the edge. She got to within five feet and stopped. Taking another deep breath, she slowly took the last couple of steps until she could peer over the ledge and watch the water flowing by far below.

Megan smiled as she stood there watching the water. Far below across the stream she saw a doe and fawn walk up to the water for a drink. Standing with her hands on her hips she surveyed nature's canvas all about her. She drank in the beauty of the moment and the world around her.

For the first time in as long as she could remember, Megan felt grateful - grateful to be alive.

CHAPTER THIRTY-THREE

Back at work, Megan found herself once again stacking canned vegetables onto a corner display. She took pride in her work. She was good at it and did it with enthusiasm.

As she grabbed another can from the box, she saw Kristy, Gloria, and Jennifer walking in her direction. Megan stood up, still holding the can.

Kristy walked right up to Megan just a couple feet from her. "Hey, Maggot. The 5K is just a few days away. You think you're ready for it?"

"We'll see won't we," replied Megan. She could tell it bothered Kristy that she wasn't intimidated anymore.

"Yeah, I guess we will," said Kristy. "Good luck." As she walked past the display, Kristy swiped her hand across the stack, sending several cans tumbling to the floor.

Mr. Mahato was at the other end of the aisle and saw what happened. He came running up to Kristy, Gloria, and Jennifer. "That's it," he said. "You girls get out of here."

Kristy answered back, "We were just -"

Sam didn't let her finish. "You were just being a word I wouldn't use in public. I won't tolerate that kind of behavior in my store. Now, please leave immediately."

The girls turned to go.

"And don't come back until you can apologize and be courteous," said Sam. He turned to Megan. "Are you alright?"

"I'm alright," said Megan. She shrugged her shoulders. "Kind of used to it."

"Shift's almost over," he said looking at his watch. "Can you make a delivery on your way home?"

"Sure," answered Megan. "Is it okay if I change into my running gear first? I wanted to get a quick run in before my mom and I have dinner tonight."

"You bet! What's on the menu?"

"Enchiladas," she said with excited anticipation. "And mine will be smothered in cheese and guacamole."

"You're making me hungry. I love enchiladas," he answered. "The groceries are all packed up. Go get changed, and I'll clean up here."

She set down the can of vegetables. "Thank you, Mr. Mahato! See you tomorrow."

"Enjoy your run and the enchiladas," he quipped. "And I'll see you tomorrow."

Megan ran to the back of the store and quickly changed into her running gear. She laced up her wildflower sneakers – that's what she called them now – and headed to the front of the store. She found the box of groceries waiting to be delivered. When she checked the name on the box, Megan paused and took a deep breath. They were going to Joanne Scissors. She picked up the box and headed out the door smiling at the thought of being able to see Jack's mom again.

CHAPTER THIRTY-FOUR

Megan found herself once again at the front door of Jack's mom's house holding a box of groceries. She took a deep breath and rang the doorbell. A moment later Joanne Scissors opened the door.

"Oh, hello again!" came the friendly greeting from Joanne. "Thank you for delivering my groceries. Come right in." Joanne stepped aside and Megan walked through the doorway.

"Thank you Mrs. Scissors."

Megan followed Jack's mom into the kitchen where she placed the box of groceries on the counter.

"You were the one who knows about my Jack," said Joanne, clearly excited to see her visitor again.

"Ah, yes, yes. I saw his memorial plaque in the school trophy case." Megan smiled as she spoke about Jack. "He was All-Conference for track in 1977. Impressive."

"He was quite the runner," answered Joanne. "But 1978 was going to be his year. He was expected to go to state. Was even one of the favorites in the long distance races. Bet you didn't know that."

"No, I didn't," said Megan smiling at the evident pride of a mother in her son.

"He even drew a big '78' on both shoes. Said it reminded him where he was headed. Kept him focused."

Megan drew a deep breath as she finally understood the meaning behind Jack's 78s. "He knew how to go all out," replied Megan.

"That he did."

"And he certainly was a handsome boy, Mrs. Scissors."

"Yes, he was," she agreed. "But so shy around the girls."

"Really?" Megan couldn't believe what she was hearing. 'Shy' was the last word she would ever use to describe Jack.

"Oh yes!" said Joanne. "He could barely spit out two words in front of a girl. Finally, with some coaxing from his father, he got up the nerve to ask one of the girls to the prom. He was so nervous. But the girl he asked was a runner like him. So he could talk to her about Steve Prefontaine 'til he was blue in the face."

"Really?!" replied Megan as she nearly laughed out loud.

"I suppose someone your age has never heard of Steve Prefontaine."

"No. I've heard of him."

"Huh," Joanne looked quizzically at Megan as she started to unpack the box of groceries. "Well then, Jack would've loved talking with you."

Megan smiled and even laughed a bit.

Joanne continued on about her son as she continued with the groceries. "So Jack asks this girl from the track team to the prom and she said yes. Well, he had no idea what to wear. So I had to take him downtown to get his suit and boutonniere." She paused for a moment. "I'm sorry. I don't mean to ramble. You probably have more important things to do than to listen to an old woman go on and on."

"No. No, that's alright," Megan replied smiling softly at the old woman. "I'd love to hear more. And there is nothing more important than what I am doing right now."

"Well, as I was saying," Joanne continued. "We were downtown getting all his stuff ready for prom. He had crossed the street to check out a new pair of running shoes in the window of Bailey's Shoe Store. It's not there anymore. Anyways, he gets done looking at the shoes and comes running back across the street to where I was standing."

Joanne stopped for a moment to take a breath. "He never saw the pickup truck."

Megan gasped.

Joanne went on, "I held him in my arms as he lay dying waiting for the ambulance.... Funny, the things a person thinks about in their last moments." Joanne stopped, grinned, and looked up at Megan. "Would you like to know what his last words to me were?"

"What?" asked Megan. She was desperate to know.

"I never got to kiss a girl."

Megan stepped back shocked by the words.

Joanne smiled and chuckled to herself. "Can you believe that? His last words, 'I never got to kiss a girl.'"

Megan turned away and wiped a tear. Turning back to Joanne she said, "He sounds like a remarkable young man."

"Oh, he was! He truly was!" agreed Joanne beaming as any proud mother would. "And now he and his father are together in heaven. Ralph passed away three years ago."

"I'm so sorry."

"That's alright. I know they're watching over me until God calls me home."

Megan took a moment to look around taking in the fact that Jack, her Jack, grew up here. "Thank you for telling me about Jack. It means more than you know."

"Oh, you are welcome, dearie," said Joanne.

Megan began to walk towards the door. "I should be going."

Joanne walked her to the door. "Well, don't be a stranger. You are welcome anytime."

Megan bent down and gave the old woman a big hug. "Thank you."

When they finished their embrace, Megan walked to her car and backed out of the driveway. Joanne Scissors waved from the doorway. Megan smiled and waved back.

CHAPTER THIRTY-FIVE

As soon as Megan got a block away from Joanne Scissors' house, she hit the gas and sped out of town to the running trail. She pulled up to the trail and jumped out of her car.

Running onto the trail, she looked one direction and then the other. No one. She turned again and called out, "Jack!"

She turned the other way and there he was in his usual running attire. They stood there for a moment staring at each other - neither saying a word. Megan was excited to see him again - even nervous.

Finally, after another moment, she took a step and then another as she walked slowly and deliberately towards him. As she got to within a couple of paces of him, Jack opened his mouth slightly as if he were about to say something. Megan quickly put her finger over her lips for him to be quiet. He obeyed and closed his mouth not saying a word.

Megan took a last step, their bodies only inches apart. They stood there staring at one another. In that moment they each held their breath. The air around them was still as if the whole world was holding its breath with them.

Neither moved, lost in the quiet joy and intimacy of being in the presence of another soul. How long they stood there, they couldn't tell. Some moments in life are measured in feelings, not seconds.

At last Megan raised herself up on her tip toes, reached up, and placed her hands around Jack's neck. Jack took in a long slow breath as he felt the touch of Megan's skin on his. His chest heaved as he felt Megan's body brush lightly against his own. Slowly bringing his arms up, he softly placed his hands on Megan's hips, his heart pounding at the nearness of her.

Megan moved her lips closer to Jack's. He closed his eyes in anticipation. She hesitated for a moment, closed her eyes, and then gently pressed her lips to his. The caress of their lips - a touch that lasted but a moment - radiated throughout her entire body. She opened her eyes to see Jack's eyes, wide with wonder, like a child upon first seeing presents under the tree on Christmas morning.

Megan slowly pulled her lips away from the boy as they exchanged a tender smile. She lowered herself until she planted her heels on the ground. Her hands slid down to Jack's shoulders as the two souls continued to take each other in with their gaze.

Jack's soft, tender smile slowly widened into a joyful grin. His reaction filled Megan's heart with a warmth and electricity that brought a similar grin to her own face. Neither of them had yet to say a word.

Savoring the moment, Jack wrapped Megan in his arms, bent down, and kissed Megan with a long, slow, tender kiss. Megan felt herself go weak in his arms. Those strong gentle arms held her safe from the world and all her fears. In the delightful intimacy of the moment, Megan found herself getting lost in Jack, forgetting that anything existed outside themselves.

Finally, Jack reluctantly pulled his lips from Megan's. Still holding each other, they stood there each one staring and smiling at the other.

"Wow," Jack whispered.

"Yeah. Wow is right," Megan whispered in reply.

He took in a deep breath and exhaled. "That was so worth waiting for."

"I'm glad you liked it."

"Did you like it too?" Jack asked his eyebrows raised with concern.

"Couldn't you tell?" she teased.

"Well, I..." Jack was suddenly unsure of himself.

Megan chuckled, "Yes. I liked it very much."

The two smiled and hugged each other tight.

Jack whispered into Megan's ear, "Thank you for coming back."

Megan moved her head back to look into Jack's eyes. "I'm sorry for being so -"

He stopped her. "No. I'm sorry I couldn't say more. My assignment was to help you, not to... all this. This... us... wasn't supposed to happen. It wasn't part of my assignment."

"It doesn't sound as romantic when you call me your assignment," she continued to tease.

"Well, someone called it in upstairs," he answered. "Said it was important to get you - and your mom - out of your funk."

Megan furrowed her brow inquisitively, "Who? Who called it in?"

Jack smiled again. "Who do you think?" He paused waiting for her to guess, but she had none. "Your dad," he finally offered.

"My dad?" Megan was in shock.

"Mmm-hmm."

A tear rolled slowly down Megan's cheek. Jack gently wiped it away with a finger.

"Your dad loves you so much," said Jack. "He watches over you every day.... He knew you and your mom needed a helping hand."

"I wish I could see him one more time." There was a sadness in her voice. "Do you think I could?"

"I don't get to make the rules on that."

"No," she answered looking down in resignation. "I suppose not."

Jack placed his hand under Megan's chin slowly lifting her head until their eyes met. "Hey. You okay?"

A warm smile slowly appeared. "Yeah. Yeah, I'm okay." She reached up and gave Jack another big hug squeezing him tight. "Thank you! Thank you so much!"

"You're welcome," he beamed. "And thank you for such a wonderfully spectacular kiss!"

"Don't mention it. You're a great kisser... for a dead guy."

They both looked wide-eyed at each other in shock at Megan's words. A moment later they burst into laughter unable to contain themselves.

When their laughter finally subsided, Jack lowered his voice and asked, "So, do you have time for one more run with this dead guy?"

"Well, I am dressed for it. I was going to go for a run after delivering groceries."

"But I'll need your shoe one more time," he said pointing at her right shoe.

Megan made no protest as she gladly took off her shoe and handed it over. Jack took out a Sharpie and scribbled for a couple of seconds, then handed it back.

Next to the words "Go all out" were two more words. Megan gasped as she whispered them aloud, "Finish it." She looked up at Jack. "Those were my dad's words."

"I know," Jack replied. "That's his reminder to you."

Megan lunged forward and gave Jack a big hug, "Thank you," she said, squeezing him tight. "Thank you, so much."

"You're welcome," he answered.

Megan stepped back and quickly put her shoe back on. She looked down smiling as she tilted the shoe to the side to see how it looked on her.

Jack looked like he was about ready to take off down the trail. "Well, if you're ready."

"Wait!" Megan caught his hand and stopped him. "Your mom. She told me about your shoes. Why you drew the 78s on them." Megan paused then said, "I'm sorry you never got a chance to go to state. You would have been great."

"Thank you." Jack answered, his voice soft and gentle. "But that's okay. God had other plans." He paused for a moment. "Anyways, it's probably time for me to get some new shoes. Something that looks to the future."

"Oh yeah?" Megan asked. "Like what?"

"I don't know. Thought about doing some hiking. Maybe a high-top."

"Wow! Expanding our horizons. I'm impressed." She replied. Megan bent her legs slightly as though about to run. "Now I'm ready."

"Hold on," he said. "One more thing. I almost forgot." Then Jack took his red headband off his head. He began to place it over Megan's head.

"What are you doing?" She asked shocked by the gesture.

"What does it look like I'm doing? I'm giving you my headband. Now you'll definitely run fast. Come on." He turned and took off down the trail.

For a moment Megan put her hands up to her head and smiled as she softly felt the worn fabric of the headband. Then she looked to see Jack running down the trail.

"Hey!" Megan cried out. But there was no stopping him, and she ran to catch up.

Soon the two were side by side moving fast down the trail. Sweat was beading on their foreheads. Jack took a lead. Megan soon caught right back up.

"I see we brought the speed today," he said with his usual cheerful smile. "Well, let's see what you've got."

Jack picked up speed, again retaking the lead. Again, Megan caught up with him.

"You know..." said Jack trying to catch his breath. "this reminds me... of something Steve... Prefontaine used to say."

Megan shook her head, "Not today," she answered with a steely resolve as she spit the words out between breaths. "You. Are. About. To. Get. Out-Prefontained."

Megan took off in a burst of speed jumping into the lead. Her legs fired like two pistons striking the ground driving her forward faster. Jack, unable to keep up, fell behind and began to fade back.

Megan found herself out in front all alone. She kept running not letting up. She figured Jack must be far behind by now, but she dared not look back. She kept her legs pumping, accelerating faster and faster.

For a moment all went silent and she heard Jack whisper as though he was right behind her, "Now you are ready."

The sound of Jack's voice so close startled Megan and she stopped abruptly. She turned to look behind her. But there was no one there. Confused she turned in a full circle. No Jack. No one.

She called out, "Jack!"

She waited. Nothing. Walking in a circle Megan put her hands on her hips catching her breath. She stopped and looked down the empty trail in the direction she had just come. She glowed with a smile and whispered, "Jack. Thank you... thank you, Jack."

Megan looked up to the sky, smiled and whispered, "Thank you, Dad."

CHAPTER THIRTY-SIX

The morning of the Arcadia Labor Day 5k found a large crowd at the starting line of the yearly spectacle. Runners from all the surrounding communities had shown up. It was always a well-attended race with numerous competitors in every age bracket.

A few yards away from the starting line Megan gathered with her mom, Riley, Trevor, and Mr. Mahato. Nervous excitement hung in the air. And Megan wore her latest fashion accessory - an old, worn-out, red headband.

Amy looked more nervous than excited. "Good luck out there," she said trying to offer words of encouragement to her daughter.

Megan smiled. "Thanks, Mom." It was such a wonderful change to hear words of encouragement from the person she loved most in this world.

Riley snuck up beside Megan and whispered in her ear, "What happened to Jack?"

"Nothing," said Megan doing her best to act like it really was nothing. "He had to go back home to his dad. He was only here for the summer."

"Sorry to hear that," replied Riley.

"It's alright," said Megan. And she meant what she said. It really was alright.

"I kind of like the headband."

"Thanks!" answered Megan as the two friends exchanged smiles.

Trevor stepped in interrupting the two, "What are you two whispering about?"

"Nothing," quipped Riley. "Just girl talk." She turned back towards Megan. "Now go kick Kristy's butt."

"Yeah! You've got this!" added Trevor. "We believe in you."

"I'll give it my best," Megan said to her friends. "But I'm not making any promises."

Mr. Mahato spoke up, "That's all you can do. Run your best and let God take care of the rest."

Megan turned and smiled at her boss grateful for his support, "Thank you, Mr. Mahato." Megan looked at everyone around her and took in a deep breath. "Well, I should head to the starting line."

Megan's high school coach, Coach Hendersen, was in attendance to see how her track and cross country athletes would perform today. She saw Megan and walked over to her. "Hey, Megan!" she shouted with her usual enthusiasm. "Glad to see you're running today!"

"Thanks, Coach," said Megan with none of her coach's enthusiasm.

"Do your best, and I'll see you at the finish line," offered the coach.

Megan nodded knowing full well that Coach Hendersen didn't expect much of a performance from her today. Actually, no one did. And she liked it that way.

Megan left her cheering section and walked to the starting line. Race time was just a few minutes away.

As she began to stretch, Megan saw Kristy, Gloria, and Jennifer nearby getting some final stretching in as well. Kristy spoke with her dad and her college coach while she stretched out getting some last-minute advice. But her posture was tense. She kept checking her watch, eyeing the competition.

Megan was close enough to hear Kristy's dad with last minute advice to his daughter. "Stick to the plan," he instructed her. "Stanford looks at early season results. So run your race."

Megan wondered what Jack's last-minute advice would be if he were here. Whatever it was, Megan was sure it would have included a Steve Prefontaine quote.

As Megan and the other runners continued their stretches, the announcer's voice echoed over the loudspeaker "Runners! Two minutes to race time!"

Megan stopped stretching and moved up closer to the starting line to find a good spot to take off from.

Kristy weaved her way through the crowd of runners until she reached Megan. "What's with the stupid headband?" asked Kristy with her usual dose of attitude.

"It's the latest fashion," answered Megan. "I'm sure everyone will be wearing them soon."

"No. It looks stupid," Kristy continued. "I'm surprised you even showed up. I thought for sure you would be off hiding somewhere."

Megan looked at her teammate and rival and smiled, "Are you scared, Kristy?"

"What?!" Kristy replied with indignation in her voice. "Of you? No way!"

Megan smiled and said with a soft assurance, "You should be."

Kristy turned away giving Megan her back. "Here you go, Maggot. This will be the only side of me you'll see today - if you're even close enough to see me at all."

Megan shrugged her shoulders and smiled as she watched Kristy rejoin Gloria and Jennifer. As Megan turned to face the course, her smile disappeared and her demeanor suddenly changed to one of steely determination. It was that same steely determination that had been growing in her all summer.

She crouched slightly into a runner's stance and waited. All the training she had been through, the backpack runs with Jack, the weightlifting at Mahato's, the radical changes in her diet - so much time and effort to get to this point. And now it all came down to this. Whatever happened, she knew she had done all she could to prepare herself for this moment. The only thing left to do was to run the race.

The other runners got set on their marks. The crowd was hushed. Megan closed her eyes for a half breath and whispered, "For you, Dad." She opened her eyes to see the road before her.

The starter pistol fired - BANG! And they were off.

CHAPTER THIRTY-SEVEN

At the sound of the gun, the crowd of runners broke from the starting line. The crowd roared. Megan burst forward out in front of the rest of the runners racing to break free of the pack.

In only a couple of minutes, she found herself alone with the top collegiate runners from nearby universities and a handful of other top-tier runners.

One of the college men glanced over, surprised to see the young girl keeping pace beside him. He smiled as he looked down at her. "Are you sure you're with the right group?" he asked.

"Are you fast?" Megan asked back.

"Yep."

"Then, I'm with the right group."

The two competitors smiled at one another and continued on.

Further back in the pack, Kristy, Gloria, and Jennifer were already far behind Megan. Kristy craned her neck trying to look over and around other runners in an attempt to find her.

"Where did she go?" asked Kristy clearly frazzled by Megan's early burst of speed.

"Don't worry about her," Gloria assured her. "At that pace she will fade in no time. Just run your race. You got this."

The three girls continued on at their current pace. But Gloria's words did nothing to put Kristy at ease.

Far ahead Megan continued her blistering pace. She still ran with the premier group of collegiate athletes. She was the only high schooler who ran with them.

With a cool end-of-summer breeze blowing gently in her face, Megan felt a surge of exhilaration as she bounded down the street. On either side onlookers cheered her and the other runners on. With each cheer, the fire and determination within Megan burned brighter.

She thought back to her first training session with Jack and how painful and difficult that had been. Now she was grateful for all the times he pushed her. She was grateful for that bag of rocks he made her carry. Compared to that this was a walk in the park.

Far back Kristy continued to search in vain for Megan. "Where is she?!" Her worry had turned to panic.

"Don't worry about her," answered Jennifer. "She'll burn herself out soon enough."

"No. This is not right," insisted Kristy. "We can't stay back like this."

"You have a game plan from one of the best college coaches in the country," argued Gloria. "Stick with the plan."

Kristy fell silent as she continued to look for Megan. Finally, she had had enough. She shook her head, "I can't stay here. I gotta catch her now or not at all."

Kristy kicked into overdrive, jumping out in front of the others with a burst of speed.

"Kristy don't!" shouted Gloria.

Kristy turned to look back at her teammates. "I gotta go!" and she was off in a blaze of speed to find Megan.

Back at the front of the race, Megan continued to push hard. She was beginning to feel the strain in her legs. Her lungs begged for more air as she did her best to give them the oxygen they desperately needed.

She remembered the words of Steve Prefontaine that Jack so often repeated. She whispered them to herself, "Take more punishment than your opponent." Those words stoked the fire within her. She began to say them over and over like a mantra in rhythm to her legs firing like twin pistons, smooth and relentless, driving her forward.

Megan looked to the side of the race course. There she saw the distance marker. She had reached the halfway point. The crowd cheered, and on she ran.

Somewhere behind Megan, Kristy was running at a lightning speed passing runners left and right. Her long strides ate up the pavement beneath her. Her breathing was heavy as her eyes focused straight ahead searching for her prey.

That prey was still far ahead. Megan could feel herself catch her second wind. The natural high of the moment and the cheering of the crowd propelled her on.

A few yards in front of Megan two young men from competing colleges were running neck and neck. Every time one tried to pull away, the other caught up. As Megan looked on, one of the runners made another attempt to get past the other. As he stepped down, the outside of his foot caught the other runner's shoe.

Both runners tripped tumbling hard to the ground just a few feet in front of Megan. She did her best to avoid the collision, but she had been following too close. She tried to hurdle the fallen runners. But at the last second one of the legs of a runner on the ground flew up in the air catching Megan's left foot.

Megan went flying forward and hit the ground hard. Her knee hit first skidding on the pavement followed by her elbow and hands.

The crowd gasped. "Are you okay?" hollered one of the spectators. Upon tumbling over, Megan got to one knee facing backwards towards the oncoming runners. Blood dripped down from her right knee and elbow.

As she looked at the oncoming runners, she spotted Kristy in the distance coming on fast. Their eyes met. A small devilish grin formed on Kristy's face. She had found her prey.

Megan's eyes flashed with that fierce fire burning within her. Without hesitation she jumped to her feet, blood and dirt streaking her skin. She turned and in an instant was running again.

"That's it! Don't give up!" yelled an enthusiastic spectator.

Another person in the crowd shouted, "Keep going!"

Megan quickly found her stride as she wiped away the last of the small gravel pebbles stuck in her scratched-up hands. Blood oozed down her leg to her ankle and into her sock and shoe. It didn't matter. She didn't feel the pain.

Both Megan and Kristy were running all out. Megan had a good forty yards on Kristy, but with those long legs Kristy was making up ground fast.

Megan glanced to the side of the course. Another distance marker showed they had just a kilometer to go. She looked back. Kristy was twenty-five yards behind and closing.

Both girls were running all out as their legs pounded the pavement beneath them. Their lungs felt ready to explode. Their clothes were drenched in sweat. But neither was about to quit. With every long stride Kristy edged closer.

Megan looked - another distance marker. Only half a kilometer to go. She turned to look back only to see Kristy right next to her. For a moment Kristy tried to give a cocky smile to Megan, but the pain in her lungs was too great. She coughed and slowed for a moment, losing a step. It took every ounce of energy to catch back up.

Only a few hundred yards remained. Both girls were running on fumes, fighting for every stride. It was all down to guts and willpower now. This is what Megan had trained for.

As they neared the finish line, the crowd began to roar.

Megan matched Kristy and then took the lead. But it didn't last long as Kristy quickly caught back up and then took her own lead.

Down by a half a stride, Megan refused to quit. Somewhere in her there had to be another gear. Jack came to mind again. She remembered him quoting Prefontaine, "To give anything less than your best is to sacrifice the gift." The words lit a spark. In an instant she found it, the next gear, and caught back up to Kristy.

The two were now neck and neck with just fifty yards to go to the finish line. Many of the spectators at the start of the race, had driven over to the finish line and were now cheering the girls on. Amy, Riley, Trevor, and Mr. Mahato cheered for Megan. Kristy's dad cheered her on while Coach Furnell and Coach Hendersen stood next to him eyes darting between the runners and their stopwatches.

"Come on, Megan! Come on!" Amy shouted at the top of her lungs.

"Go Megan!!! Woo hoo!!!" yelled Riley and Trevor.

Kristy's dad and Coach Furnell looked on in surprise - unnerved even - as they watched their track star in a desperate battle with a few yards to go.

Kristy's dad cheered her on, but his words were muted meant more for himself than anyone else. "Come on, Kristy! Go!"

In the final twenty yards, both girls gave one final push - legs burning, lungs ready to burst. Megan gave every last bit of energy left in her worn-out body as she hurtled her body forward. Kristy lunged forward in one final stride as they crossed the finish line together.

As they broke the tape, both girls collapsed to the ground, gasping for breath, the crowd erupting into cheers all around them.

CHAPTER THIRTY-EIGHT

Megan and Kristy lay on the ground next to each other gasping for air. Amy, Riley, Trevor, and Sam rushed to Megan's side. Kristy's dad and Coach Furnell ran to help their athlete.

Once on her feet, Kristy took a couple of steps as her dad and coach held her up. For Megan a first aid kit was pulled out by a race volunteer as they bandaged up her knee and elbow.

"That was absolutely incredible!" Amy uttered in amazement as the volunteer continued to bandage her elbow. "I am so proud of you," she said emphasizing each word slowly.

"Thanks, Mom!" Megan smiled in spite of the pain of the hydrogen peroxide being applied to her knee.

Megan looked up at her friends standing over her. Her face beamed with pride in what she had just accomplished. Gratitude for all these people in her life who loved her and cared for her filled her heart.

"Wow," was all Riley could say. "I... I've never seen anything like that!"

Trevor chimed in, "I had no idea you were going to do something like that. I'm pretty sure you have bragging rights over my mini-putt victory." Megan laughed out loud at that.

Sam Mahato was stoic yet smiling as well. He said softly, "Well done, Megan. Well done."

"Thank you, Mr. Mahato. I couldn't have done it without you... and all those crazy weights you set up for me."

That got Sam finally laughing as well. "Don't tell anyone, or they'll all be coming to my store to work out."

As they all laughed and celebrated, a few feet away Kristy and her small entourage were a more serious sort.

Kristy's dad was as intense as ever, "Good job out there. That was really good."

"Thanks," gasped Kristy still struggling for air.

"You were really fast out there," added Coach Furnell. "Really fast."

"When are they going to say who won?" asked Kristy's dad. He shouted over to the official timekeeper's table, "Hey! Who won the 15- to 19-year-old girls' category?"

The entire crowd turned to the official timekeeper sitting in front of a small monitor. She looked up and shouted "Too close to call! We are checking the camera."

A hush went over the crowd. Riley turned to Megan, "Doesn't matter. You showed Kristy. Heck, you showed everybody. It was incredible."

Megan said nothing. She just smiled as she stood there all bandaged up proud of how she had run - proud that she didn't quit when she fell.

The crowd murmured waiting for the result. "Well!" shouted Mr. McDermott again getting annoyed by the delay. "Who won?"

After a few more seconds of the race officials conferring, the head of the racing association stood up to make the announcement. The entire crowd fell silent. "The photo finish shows the winner of the girls 15- to 19-girls' division is..." He paused for effect and then, "Kristy McDermott!"

There were several cheers and even a few disappointed groans. The crowd knew what a remarkable performance

Megan's run was. And word had spread that she had fallen and still almost won.

Kristy's dad gave a big fist pump and held up his daughter's arm in victory. Coach Furnell patted her on the back to congratulate her.

Mr. Mahato put his hand on Megan's head and ruffled her hair. "Don't you dare get down on yourself. You were magnificent."

Megan smiled, "Thank you. And don't worry. I won't."

At that moment Megan heard a strange guttural sound coming from Kristy's direction. She looked over to see Kristy vomiting all over the ground.

Megan looked over to Mr. Mahato. "I know what that feels like."

Kristy wiped her mouth and after a few more seconds was finally able to stand up straight. She stood still, catching her breath.

Her dad pumped his fist a couple of times celebrating his victory. He then turned to her and said, "Let's go home, Champ."

But Kristy didn't move.

"You coming?" he asked, reaching for her arm.

Kristy shook him off. "Hold on."

She left her dad and made her way through the crowd to Megan. The smugness was gone. So was the usual swagger. When she reached Megan the two girls stood there for a moment staring at each other.

"You pushed me," said Kristy, her voice raspy. "I've never run like that in my life. You're good. Really good."

Megan blinked, unsure how to respond. "Thanks," she said. "You're really good too."

"I needed that. Needed you," Kristy continued. "I just wish I'd figured that out sooner."

Megan nodded. "We both had stuff to figure out."

Kristy managed a smile, "Well thanks." She looked down at

Megan's shoes. "You always did have cool shoes. Still not sure about the headband, though."

The girls laughed together - something they had not done in years.

Kristy continued. "You know if those guys hadn't tripped you up, you would have won for sure."

"Maybe," answered Megan. "We'll find out for sure this cross-country season."

"Yes, we will," answered Kristy smiling at her worthy opponent.

Coach Hendersen, who had been timing the race, was confirming the results with the race officials. After speaking with the head official, she came running over to Megan and Kristy. "Do you realize what both of you just did?"

The girls looked at their coach confused by her words.

"Huh? What?" Megan asked.

"You both broke the state record! Both of you! By four seconds! I've never seen anything like it!" Coach Hendersen looked completely flabbergasted.

"Well coach," said Kristy. "Sometimes it just takes a little friendly competition to get us going."

Megan looked puzzled at Kristy. "Friendly?"

Kristy turned to Megan, "You heard me. I'll see you in school tomorrow... Megan."

She said her name. Her actual name. Megan couldn't believe it. That was probably the closest she would get to an actual apology from Kristy. Megan smiled once more, "Yeah, see you in school, Kristy."

Kristy slowly walked back to her dad holding her stomach as though she might throw up again.

Coach Furnell ran over to Coach Hendersen and handed her his card. "Give me a call," he said. "I know a number of coaches at some of the top track and cross-country colleges in the nation. They'll want to keep tabs on these two."

Coach Hendersen took the card and nodded as she put it in

her pocket. "I'll certainly give you a call. I'm expecting big things from both of them."

Amy stepped in front of her daughter staring her square in the face. "You did it. You really did it. I am so proud of you." Her eyes were getting teary.

"Thanks, Mom," said Megan as her eyes got teary as well.

They hugged each other and held each other tight.

"I love you so much," whispered Amy into Megan's ear. "And your dad would be so proud."

"He is," whispered Megan. "I know he is."

As they continued to hold each other, Megan looked off in the distance. There, standing alongside the curb, she saw Jack. He stood there in T-shirt, tube socks, and short shorts. He smiled at Megan with that ever-optimistic smile and pointed down at his shoes.

Megan looked down to see Jack wearing new shoes. The old 78s were replaced by a pair of brand new, retro-styled high-tops ready for hiking. She had to admit the boy had good taste in shoes.

Megan gave Jack a thumbs up and returned the smile as she let herself enjoy this last moment with the boy who had taught her so much - how to run, how to love, and how to live again. Her gratitude for the boy and his impact on her life almost overwhelmed her.

And then she saw him. Her eyes opened wide and a tear ran down her face as she saw a man step from behind Jack and stand at his side. It was her dad. He stood there smiling. Tears ran down Megan's cheeks.

Megan's dad mouthed the words, "I love you."

Megan mouthed the same words back to him. "I love you."

A moment later Amy released her daughter from her embrace. She looked down at her daughter in tears. "Are you okay?" Amy asked.

"Yeah," said Megan wiping a tear away. "I'm perfect."

"Ready to go home?" Amy asked.

"Yeah. Let's go home."

Megan looked back to the curb. Her dad and Jack were gone. She looked up to the sky and smiled and then turned to walk away with her friends. Riley took Megan by one arm and her mom took her by the other. Trevor grabbed Riley's other arm, and Sam walked up to Amy and offered her his arm. She took it, and the five of them walked off together.

As they walked off Megan thought again of all Jack had taught her - about living life to the full and taking chances. As they continued to walk away, Megan suddenly spoke up, "Hey Trevor!"

"Yeah?" he answered surprised by the sudden outburst.

"What are you doing Saturday night?"

"Me? Nothing planned."

"Up for a burger and a movie?" asked Megan.

"Um... Sure!" a shocked Trevor replied.

"Great! It's a date!" answered Megan with a newfound self-assurance. "Pick me up at 6:00."

"Ah... Okay. It's a date!" Trevor beamed.

Riley turned to Megan and whispered, "It's about time."

"Well, you were right," said Megan, grinning. "He is cute"

The two girls laughed.

Trevor spoke up for the entire gang to hear, "Did you see Kristy throwing up? That was so gross!"

Megan and the others laughed out loud as they walked away. In the pure joy and bliss of the moment she remembered Jack's words to her. "Doing what's hard - that's where life's greatest blessings are waiting for us."

In this moment, Megan knew those words to be true. She knew it with every fiber of her being. And she knew that for the rest of her life she would always be grateful for the many blessings she had been graced with during that summer of running with Jack Scissors.

THE END

THE STORY BEHIND THE STORY

Running with Jack Scissors didn't start as a book.

The idea was born in a season of loss. It started as a screenplay with the hope it might one day become a film that moves people, lifts them up, and leaves them a little better than before.

Just five emails into sending it out, something incredible happened: The Boylan Sisters — Alexandra and Andrea, the award-winning team behind five inspiring Gen Z films — read the script and said yes. They're now on board to direct, bringing their amazing crew with them.

That left one big question:

How do we make this movie without giving away its heart to a studio or spending years chasing investors?

The answer was to flip the model — and do it together.

No "pledge and hope" crowdfunding. Instead, we'd create merch you can enjoy right now, with profits going straight into making the film.

Since Running with Jack Scissors is about running, the first thing we made was obvious: shoes.

Not just any shoes — limited-edition 1970s-style retro sneakers inspired by the ones Jack and Megan wear in the story.

Fun. Bold. Collectible. Limited Edition. When they're gone, they're gone.

At Storypop.studio you can:

1. Grab your favorite sneakers (and other exclusive merch)

2. Vote on cast choices and behind-the-scenes decisions

3. Become an affiliate partner and earn 20% commission + bonuses

4. And maybe even join us on set or walk the red carpet

Yes, really! The Top 25 partners will attend the premiere and could even be cast as extras in the movie.

If this story meant something to you, I'd be honored to finish it together.

Visit www.Storypop.Studio and help bring Running with Jack Scissors to the big screen.

See you at the premiere.

— DJ Hellman

www.ingramcontent.com/pod-product-compliance
Lightning Source LLC
Chambersburg PA
CBHW050340110726
47899CB00007B/2578